THE HEART OF MARS

Paul grew up in Newton Aycliffe in County Durham, and was educated at Woodham Comprehensive and Lancaster University. He was a lecturer in Creative Writing and English Literature at UEA for seven years, running their famous MA course, and then did the same job at MMU in Manchester for a further seven years. He now writes fulltime at home in Levenshulme, near Manchester, where he lives with his partner Jeremy Hoad.

Paul has published a number of YA novels – *Strange Boy* (2002), *Exchange* (2006, shortlisted for the Book Trust Teen Book Award and longlisted for the Carnegie), *Diary of a Dr Who Addict* (2010 shortlisted for the Leeds Book Prize) and for younger readers – *Hands up!* (2003), *Twin Freaks* (2007), *The Ninnies* (2012). He has also published five original Doctor Who novels with BBC books, and over twenty original Doctor Who audiobooks / full cast dramas produced by Big Finish Productions and BBC Audio/Audiogo. He has written for almost all the living Doctors!

THE HEART OF MARS

PAUL MAGRS

Firefly

First published in 2018
by Firefly Press
25 Gabalfa Road, Llandaff North, Cardiff, CF14 2JJ
www.fireflypress.co.uk

A CIP catalogue record of this book is available from the British Library.

ISBN 978-1-910080-58-0

*This book has been published with the support of the
Welsh Books Council.*

Typeset by: Elaine Sharples

Printed and bound by: Pulsio SARL

1

'You can do it, Peter. I know you can. It's not a massive jump.'

He was frozen to the spot. All his limbs had locked and he was standing there, staring at me. He couldn't move an inch.

'There's nothing to it,' I told him. 'Look! Karl did it. Karl jumped easy.'

Karl was at my feet, wagging his tail and doing his best to look encouraging. He'd sailed through the air to land on this muddy bank, easy as anything.

'Karl's got cybernetic legs,' Peter pointed out. 'Of course he can jump.'

'But so can you! What's the matter with you?'

I was goading him on purpose, but I was starting to lose my temper, too.

'All right…' Peter gritted his teeth. 'Stop yelling at me…'

He looked down at the filthy water.

'Don't look at it!'

It was a hellish sight. Thick purple, oozing mud. Bursting with swamp gas bubbles. It looked like it'd poison you dead if you dipped just one toe in. Looking down was a big mistake. Plus the jump was further than I was saying.

'I'll grab you!' I promised him. 'Just jump!'

He'd made the first few jumps across the swamp okay. From island to island, dotting our way from bank to bank. But something had made him lose his nerve this time.

'We don't have time for messing about, Peter. We gotta find some dry land before night falls.'

'I know that,' he said. 'But … they're looking at me.'

'Who are?'

And then I saw them.

What I'd thought were black bubbles on the filthy water – they weren't bubbles. They were eyes. They blinked at us. Gold and black and nasty-looking. And they were watching Peter. Two pairs, three pairs. More were surfacing as I watched. Five, six. They were coming to stare at him, hungrily. Ten, twelve. How many more? The more I looked around the more I could see. What kind of creatures were these, anyway, with gleaming eyes, each as big as my head?

'D-don't look at them! They aren't there!'

'Yes, they are,' said Peter. 'You know they are. And they've been watching us ever since we came to this hideous place…'

Perhaps he was right. Ever since we arrived in the swamps there'd been that feeling of something watching us, studying us. And now we could see them. Dozens of eyes, emerging from the purple mud.

Karl the cat-dog barked suddenly, loudly. He snapped his tiny teeth.

And that's what did it. Without thinking about it a second more Peter thrust himself forward, his arms windmilling clumsily. He tumbled headfirst towards us, just missing the muddy bank right in front of me.

He yelled and I darted forward to grab him while Karl jumped and barked. All three of us were engulfed in the stinking fog as I pulled him free of the mud and it felt like an eternity before we collapsed in a relieved heap on solid ground. Well, mostly solid ground.

'You did it!'

I was laughing with relief and Peter started laughing too.

'Let's get right away from those things,' I said. I glanced back, only to see that the eyes were vanishing once more under the surface.

We hurried on, keeping as far from the soupy waters as we could. Neither of us were used to terrain like this. Peter was a city boy and had never seen a place so primitive or inhospitable. I grew up on the Martian prairie, where everything was dusty and dry, of course. Water never stood still long enough to grow mouldy and slimy. And it never had *eyes* in it, that was for sure.

But this was where we had to be. When we'd learned that we had to go to the swamplands of the north, I admit my heart sank. I've never heard anything good about swamps or bogs. But there was no other way. This was where my ma and my sister Hannah had been sent. This was where they were last seen. And we had to go after them.

We found a relatively dry hollow by the base of several ancient, leathery trees. I dished out the chewy green cubes of food we'd been given.

'These are disgusting,' Peter pulled a face.

'When I was a kid on the prairie, these were a great delicacy,' I told him. 'Only the Oldsters had these, left over from their days aboard the Starships, when they came from Earth.'

'I suppose you'd have eaten anything on that prairie of yours,' he smiled.

'Hey, when the crops were good, we ate well. But sometimes we were glad of Grandma's supply of space cubes…'

We chewed in silence for a while, and I was thinking about my former life at the Homestead. It seemed like a million years ago now. Further than any Starship could travel. Those years with Da and Ma and Grandma, Al and Hannah were very distant. None of us was together anymore.

But there was no use dwelling on that. That was the whole reason for my quest. I was reuniting my family, whatever it took.

'I suppose we're lucky to have any food at all,' Peter said, looking worried he might have upset me by bringing up the past.

4

'At least we don't have to hunt and eat swamp creatures,' I told him, and he went a funny colour.

By then we'd been two days inside the swamp. I didn't know how far it went on. It might be forever. It could be we'd get stuck wandering here for the rest of our lives. We had three days of cubes and no other kind of plan. We had just been told: head north. That's the way we sent your ma and sister.

They had been sent as sacrifices. That's what the people of Ruby's town had told us.

It was still shocking to think about.

Ruby was my grandma's oldest living friend. She had settled in a town that looked so much like Our Town on the prairie, that when we got there Ruby's town almost felt like home. But everything about her had changed. When we'd found her in her new town Ruby had gone crazy and she had locked us all up. The truth had come out. She and her people were crazy-religious; they worshipped creatures they called the Ancient Ones. Finally she'd admitted that they had taken Hannah and Ma as offerings to these mysterious beings in the swamp.

Ruby used to be like a friendly old aunt to us kids. How could she do such a thing? But I'd seen so many strange things in recent times. It was amazing how much strangeness you could absorb. I just had to keep my mind on our quest. Finding my family, and going home.

I could see from the look on his face that Peter was thinking along similar lines.

'Our plan's quite simple, isn't it?' he smiled.

'Since when did I go in for elaborate, foolproof plans?' I laughed.

'We're just heading north and hoping for the best, aren't we?'

I nodded. 'Of course. What else can we do?'

'I thought so,' he said, and nodded, still smiling.

Maybe we should have been more worried or scared. I dunno. Somehow when we were together things didn't seem so bad. I knew I could depend on him.

Karl darted off into the undergrowth then. He surprised us both by bringing back a small, blue, hairless creature he'd caught. He ate it in two bites, smacking his lips. Peter was appalled. 'Karl!'

But how long would it be before we were all eating creatures like that?

Night came oozing and crawling greasily through the swamp, bringing more of that reeking, yellow fog. We bedded down to sleep with our coats over us, huddled in the hollow between the roots of the trees.

For a while I thought I was sleeping. Then I heard Peter saying, 'Can you hear those noises?'

'Yeah.'

'I thought I was dreaming.'

'No, it's voices. I can hear voices…'

Distorted and sometimes lost inside all the night-time noise, there were definitely words and sentences being formed out there somewhere in the swamplands. People were calling out to each other. They sounded … not friendly, exactly. But at least they were alive and intelligent. That's what I was telling myself, anyhow.

I'd known Peter for less than a year. It was hard to believe that this rangy, unkempt boy hadn't been in my life longer than that. I'd met him when he was busking in the City Inside at Christmas time. He was playing a miniature harp, just like the one Ma used to play. It was what drew me to him. There he was, in the marketplace, with his scrappy cat-dog Karl, making this beautiful music.

We'd become friends and he showed me the secret and illegal place where he lived, a system of tunnels underneath the City park.

It was such a strange time for me. I was only just settling into the City Inside, a place I'd never have chosen to be. I'd wandered out of the desert, having lost half of my family and here I was in this amazing place that we'd never even known existed. It was all green glass towers and domes, and red snow was tumbling out of the sky…

So much had happened very quickly. My brother Al settled in quite easily and got taken up by one of the richest, ruling families. I was at a loose end, of course. Even our robotic sunbed Toaster found a small community of Servo-Furnishings to befriend.

But it was me who discovered something marvellous about the City Inside.

It was where all the Disappeared people turned up.

That was what we called them, back on the prairie. The Disappeared. They vanished in the middle of the night. They were taken from their beds; they were snatched from their homes.

I had seen the ghostly, giggling creatures who'd taken them away. I'd watched them dancing down the dusty red road.

And they had Disappeared my da and my grandma. When that happened the shock and the grief were terrible. I was always a daddy's girl. When he'd gone it would have been easy to give up and wait for the ghosts to come and take us all. But instead we had taken action. I had led the rest of my family – Ma, Hannah, Al and Grandma – away from Our Town, in search of somewhere safer to live.

On our journey, we were all split up and we'd lost Hannah and Ma. Only Al, Toaster and I ended up in the gleaming and mysterious City Inside. I'd made friends with Peter and Karl. I'd made an enemy of the Authorities who seemed to want to pick my brains about everything I had learned in my life on the prairie.

But most amazing of all, I'd found Da and Grandma, living in a tiny flat together in the very middle of the City.

Half my family was back together!

I didn't know how, and I didn't understand why. I still didn't know how it all pieced together. But I was glad. And now I was determined that I was going to find Hannah and Ma too. Hannah and Ma were left behind and so I'd returned to the wilderness to find them.

It had taken another huge journey and all kinds of dangers and now we were venturing into terrain I'd never even seen before.

But I felt we were getting closer to the end of the journey. In the dark of this sweltering, noisy jungle, we were lost and unnerved, but I felt sure that we were coming to the heart of it all.

I was woken up all at once by a hideous noise. It was a crashing, splintering noise of branches being smashed. It was a wrenching, thrashing noise of something hauling itself out of the murky waters of the swamp. I was on my feet in a flash. Both Peter and Karl were awake too, looking as scared as I felt.

The whole ground seemed to be lurching under our feet. And the noise was getting louder. Whatever it was, it was coming closer.

By now it was day. Golden, shimmering light came through the heavy branches of the trees and that was a blessing at least. We could at least see what we were facing.

Peter said, 'Lora, look…!'

Karl was so horrified he forgot how to bark.

It was all the eyes. They had followed our trail through the swamp and tracked us down.

It turned out that those dozens of black and golden eyes did not belong to dozens of separate creatures after all. Each pair was swaying at the end of a golden tentacle, and each tentacle was attached to the shapeless head of a single massive, swaying creature. A creature covered in swamp muck and slime. A creature that was crashing purposefully through the trees, looking for us. It loomed tall as the trees. All those eyes on stalks were blazing with golden fire.

'Keep still, Peter,' I hissed.

The eyes swivelled in mid-air and looked at me and then at him.

Underneath all the swamp slime and scum the body seemed to be made of scarred and knotted bark. Its hands were huge and the wooden fingers creaked as they moved towards us.

'Not many of your kind come here,' the creature said.

We both jumped in shock. It spoke our language! The voice was huge and shattering. It was hard to see where it came from but the noise filled our heads.

Karl found his voice and yapped furiously.

'Who … w-what are you?' I mustered my courage and spoke up.

He trained his many eyes on my face. 'I am Goomba.'

10

When he said the name it echoed through the humid air.

'What do you want?' asked Peter.

'I am the guardian of the swamp,' he said. 'I am here to command you to go back the way you came.'

Peter looked at me. He hissed, 'How are we going to get past him? He's huge!'

'What will you do if we don't go back?' I said, sounding as brave as I could.

The eyes quivered with fury. 'I will smash you to smithereens!' With that he raised up both massive hands, trailing rooty tendrils that lashed around his head, and he brought them crashing down into the swamp water. We were knocked off our feet and drenched instantly.

'I think he means it,' said Peter.

He could have killed us in an instant. But he hadn't yet. We had a chance to communicate with him.

Suddenly I knew what I must ask him. I stood up and, gagging at the stench of brackish mud, I took a step closer.

'If you're the guardian of this place, have you seen my mother? She looks like me, only twenty years older. And my sister, Hannah, who's very small? They came this way. They were sent this way as sacrifices. The humans of Ruby's town back beyond the desert, sent them here. They sent them as tribute to the people they call the Ancient Ones…'

Goomba had apparently been listening with great care

to my words. When I said the phrase 'Ancient Ones' he became very agitated. His multiple eyes flashed greenish-gold and whipped about on the end of those tentacles. He cried out in rage and the sodden, boggy ground quaked in response to his anger.

'So do the Ancient Ones really exist, then?' Peter spoke up bravely. 'They're not just some legend of the townsfolk?'

'Stop!' cried Goomba in fury. Those vast hands of his went up again and I was afraid he was really going to bring them down and smash us like he'd promised. 'You human children don't understand! They will hear you in their sleep. Your words will penetrate their slumbers! You mustn't wake the Sleepers under the swamp.'

'But we must,' I said. 'If that's where Ma and Hannah have gone. We must wake up these Ancient Ones and ask them.'

'You don't want to wake them.'

'I need to know where my ma is,' I said, staring determinedly back, not sure if I was scared of him or not any more. 'And I think you know. You're the guardian. You've got all those eyes. I think you saw my family. Won't you tell me where they are?'

The many eyes shivered violently, and he held up those wooden hands again like he wanted to swat me out of existence. His arms and eyes, tentacles and all, began to sway menacingly towards me…

'No. I cannot tell you. You must go back the way you

came. Leave the swamp tonight, Lora Robinson. Leave at once!'

'How do you know my name?'

But the creature was turning away from us and, with surprising speed, he slipped away under the swamp waters.

Next thing we knew, there were bullets screaming over our heads and zinging into the tree trunks. Peter and I flung ourselves on to the ground.

Blam blam blam. More gunfire through the trees.

Bullets sizzled through the murky air. Then, just as abruptly as it had started, the gunfire stopped. Two figures came lurching through the golden mist. A dumpy human form and a bulky robot.

I could hardly believe what I was seeing. It was Grandma, grinning, with a rifle held aloft, plus Toaster, her sunbed, who looked delighted to see us.

2

'Good job we came after you,' Grandma cackled as she cleaned her rifle. 'I should have known you kids would get yourselves straight into danger…'

This wasn't quite fair, I pointed out, since Peter and I had spent almost a week trekking across the desert by ourselves, managing quite well, thanks very much. And we'd made it so far into the swamp before meeting Goomba and, besides, I think I had managed to pacify him a little. He wasn't really going to smash us into smithereens, I was sure. I didn't actually need Grandma and Toaster dashing in to the rescue…

'Ha! Yeah, but you're pleased to see us, all the same, ain't you?' Grandma shouted. Now she was hugging Peter hard and slapping him on the back.

Back in Ruby's town Grandma had been close to despair. Her oldest friend had turned out to be crazy and had threatened to kill us all and, as a result, much of Grandma's life force had seemed to be gone. But she'd changed in the short time since we'd seen her. She was full of vitality again.

'We couldn't let you get lost in this swamp,' she said,

picking up a startled Karl and dancing him around on the squelching ground. She looked like a crazy lady, with her wild white hair and her faded clothes and weather-beaten, sun-cracked face. 'I couldn't just sit around in that backward town with all the rest of them, waiting and hoping that you'd come back. And no way was I going back to that City Inside. So all I could do, I decided, was fix up Toaster and get him to train his sensors on following you!'

We all stared at Toaster, our family's trusty sunbed. He was gleaming, polished, as good as brand new. In just a matter of days Grandma had put him back together better than ever. Toaster wasn't just a robot to us. He was a member of our family. Before we'd left the town, while we stood frozen in horror, he'd been battered and bludgeoned by the crazy congregation in Ruby's so-called church. His mind had been scattered and shattered within his buckled metal body.

But Grandma had managed to restore him! Sometimes I forgot how skilled a technician she had once been. It seemed that she had forgotten none of her skills.

Toaster nodded proudly. 'I am completely back to my optimum level of functioning. Thanks to your grandma, Margaret Estelle Robinson, my oldest friend on this planet, my entire memory and personality have been returned to me.'

'Really?' I grinned at him and rushed over to hug his metal body. 'Toaster, that's wonderful news.'

15

For too long before Ruby's town he hadn't been himself. He had been taken over by the Authorities of the City Inside and his original, friendly, loyal personality had been – we thought – utterly erased. That sunbed who had helped us for all those years on the prairie and in the Homestead, who had trekked with us through the wilderness as we looked for a new home – he had been with us every step of the way, never questioning that his place was wherever the Robinson family's fortunes took them. But then, thanks to the rulers of the City Inside, we thought we had lost our friendly Toaster forever. We had found ourselves having to get used to a cold and brusque new sunbed, and we had been in mourning for a friend we'd thought could never return.

'I am ashamed of myself,' the old sunbed admitted. 'I was lost inside myself and couldn't speak out. I was shouting and calling, but it was like someone else was in control of my brain…' For a few moments he looked troubled and a crackle of interference clouded his screens. 'But here I am now, fully restored. And we are all together again, ready to make plans.'

We spent some time eating a breakfast of spiced cakes and coffee that Grandma had been saving for our reunion. It was amazing how even that stinking corner of the swamp seemed almost homely now we had something decent to eat and drink. We talked and made plans about the upcoming days. Toaster shared the few sketchy aerial maps he had compiled of the northlands, and Peter and I described our encounter with Goomba.

'We detected a large creature in your vicinity,' said Toaster. 'It must have been very frightening for you.'

'He was pretty scary. At first anyway,' said Peter.

'But he seemed even more frightened of anyone waking up the Ancient Ones,' I pointed out.

'That's our first confirmation that the people we are searching for actually exist,' Grandma frowned. Her face looked more seamed and crumpled than ever. And yet there was more vitality in it than I'd seen before. 'The Ancient Ones.'

Peter said anxiously, 'Goomba told us we shouldn't even talk about them, in case they might hear us and wake…'

Grandma rolled her eyes. 'We want them to wake up, don't we? We want to know all about them. We want them to give us back Lora's ma and Hannah.'

It was good to hear Grandma so determined and clear about what we should do next. For most of my life I had been used to her freaking out and doing just the wrong things. Smashing up the Homestead while we were out, or kicking up a storm when it just wasn't necessary. It was something I had noticed recently – Grandma was less erratic and crazy when times were truly dangerous.

Toaster said, 'Going to meet these so-called Ancient Ones might be the most hazardous adventure we have embarked on yet.'

I started thinking about the pictures in that weird church-like building back in Ruby's town. They'd shown leaping flames and strange creatures in underground caverns. There'd been pictures of humans and winged Martians being fed to those flames. If all that stuff was true, what kind of dangers were we walking so willingly into?

We set off again, soon after breakfast. None of us wanted to hang around by those waters, just in case the golden eyes of Goomba came lifting out of the surface again, and this time he really did want to smash us to smithereens.

'There'll be other guardians, I imagine,' Grandma said, cocking her rifle and setting off through the trees. 'And there'll be other creatures in these swamps, even more horrible than Goomba...' She seemed to be enjoying imagining the dangers that might be lurking ahead.

Peter and Karl walked alongside me and the going was easier with Toaster there. His strong metal arms whizzed and sliced and tore through the clinging jungle vines that we were now pushing through. The Servo was tireless, as we well knew, and it saved us a lot of work, cutting our way through the undergrowth, inch by inch.

The deeper we went into the swamp the hotter and darker it became. It must have been the middle of the day but it was gloomy in here. The air was heavy and green all about us. We had to shed layers of our loose desert clothing, but we soon found out it was a bad idea to expose any skin. The insects were huge – the size of bats – and they would bite any flesh they could get to. Soon we had lumpy red blisters that itched like mad, and the buzzing noises never seemed to stop.

'I'm not sure about your grandma,' Peter said, sidling close to me.

'What do you mean?'

'She was pretty close to Dean Swiftnick in the City Inside,' he said. 'What if she's working for the Authorities now? What if they're sending her this way on a kind of mission?'

Peter was always suspicious about the higher-up folk in the City Inside. I was, too, especially after some of the tribulations we'd been through. But still I said, 'I don't think you've got to worry about Grandma. I reckon you're just being paranoid.'

'But she's had her head messed around with, and so has Toaster,' Peter said. 'I'm just saying, we've got to be careful who we trust.'

Well, I'd always known it was dodgy trusting Grandma. As far as I was concerned, the old lady had always been crazy. But at least, so far, she hadn't turned traitor on us. She was on our side, I was sure.

That evening we heard the voices again. We sat huddled together, eating our supper, and listening hard.

'There are other folk living here,' Grandma said. 'We

should find them. We gotta talk to them, whoever they are.'

'But … they might be dangerous,' Peter said. 'What kind of people live in a terrible place like this?'

'We gotta find them,' said Grandma steadfastly and I thought to myself: yeah, maybe she does know something we don't. She had that look about her. I saw her exchange a glance with Toaster just then. Perhaps they *were* up to something, those two.

The next day saw us travelling further into the murksome and stinking swamplands. The going became harder as the trees were larger here, and more closely packed together. Fleshy, rubbery vines hung down thicker than ever. There was also a nasty creeper with thorns that grew underfoot.

All through that day, as we inched deeper into the jungle the distant, unknown voices became more distinct. Bellowing shouts of bravado. Jeering. Laughter.

Grandma nodded mysteriously.

'Who are they?' Peter asked her.

'I don't think they're anyone to be alarmed about,' she said.

I wasn't too sure about that. They sounded wild and dangerous to me.

Toaster was using his sensors to tune into them. 'We are quite close to a settlement,' he said, suddenly, pausing as if to sniff the air.

'Maybe I'll go in first, and alone,' said Grandma. 'And do our talking for us.'

'What?' I couldn't believe what she was saying. 'You can't go first. You're…'

'An old lady? With one leg and only one eye?' She crowed with laughter. 'Yeah, I'm not as helpless as all that, Lora, as you well know.'

'Whoever these people are, we face them together,' I said steadfastly.

'They aren't people,' said Toaster. 'Not as such.'

I was about to ask him what he meant when Karl let out a volley of barks. Peter picked him up swiftly, muffling his noise. 'Look,' he hissed at the rest of us.

Sure enough, about a hundred yards up ahead, there was a glade and there was movement. Someone or something was moving through the trees. There was more of that loud, raucous shouting.

'Bandits,' said Grandma.

'What?' I gasped.

I stared with the others and was astonished to see – not human beings, nor Martians, nor hybrids nor any other kind of organic creatures. What we saw were Servo-Furnishings, ambling through the swamp and talking noisily among themselves. Boxy, wooden, lumbering machines. Some of them were metallic, others were painted. Each of them seemed to have different functions. One was covered with light bulbs and cast a golden halo about himself. Another had a glass front and was filled with ice. A third shape bristled with evil-looking weaponry and had a stuffed beast's head with antlers and glassy eyes that swivelled madly around.

All of the machines were covered in lichen and mould. They looked exactly like furniture that had been left out for years in a treacherous swampy land. Fronds of shaggy moss hung from their artificial limbs and their watery innards creaked and sloshed.

'Servos?' Peter gasped. 'That's who lives out here? They're the *bandits*?'

Grandma nodded grimly. 'Exactly. And we're gonna need their help, I reckon.' Without any further ado she pushed forward through the jungle vines and presented herself before the Servo-Furnishings.

'We come in peace,' she said.

'Oh, my goodness,' Peter gasped. 'She's brave! And I bet she's going to say, "take me to your leader".'

Which is precisely what Grandma did say.

The swamp bandits were staring at her in some surprise and when the rest of us emerged from the trees they became suspicious and started muttering amongst themselves. Where were these strangers coming from? What was going on?

They were particularly alarmed at the sight of Toaster. How smart and gleaming he seemed next to their dingy, mould-spattered casings.

'This woman is an extremely important person,' he said, in his grandest voice. 'She is one of the few Earth women left alive on Mars, and you people are commanded to obey her, just as I do.'

The bandits were still muttering to each other under their breath.

'I don't like this,' Peter said. 'Look at the weapons they've got. If they turned on us, we wouldn't stand a chance.'

'I know.' I grabbed his arm and ruffled Karl's fur. 'I'd have preferred to stay away from them…'

But Grandma had made the decision for us, and she was looking mighty pleased with herself.

The Servo that was sporting a bright array of old-fashioned light bulbs stepped forward on his delicate feet. 'We would be honoured to deliver you to Bandit Town.' He gave a stiff bow.

Grandma hurried forward. 'Who will we find in charge?' she needed to know. 'Tell me, please. Who is your leader?'

'All your questions will be answered soon,' said the Servo with all the lights. His fellows were moving forward now and ushering the rest of us back the way their party had come.

'But you must tell me,' Grandma said in a quavering voice. Her true feelings were coming out now. To me she sounded half afraid, half excited. 'Tell me, please. Is Thomas still alive?'

As we followed the weird robots through the trees to the settlement known as Bandit Town I was trying to get over my shock.

'Who is this Thomas?' Peter wanted to know. 'I don't understand, Lora. How could your grandma know anyone living out this way, in the middle of the swamps? Has she been here before?'

That was a good question. I didn't know whether Grandma had ever been this way before in her life. She certainly didn't seem familiar with the damp and nasty terrain.

But I did know who Thomas was.

'You actually think Thomas could still be alive?' I asked her, tugging on her sleeve.

'We're a long-lived family,' she said. 'We're all pretty tough. I've always felt somehow that he was alive. I felt like I knew Thomas was still here, somewhere on Mars. And the few rumours I heard pointed to the swamp. King of the bandits. My very own brother. Fancy that! The thing is, it was all a long time ago. I didn't want to set up false hope. But all I know is that if the stories are true, then Thomas will surely help us find our family. He and his people. His tribe of bandits. I'm sure I'll be able to get him to help us. How can he refuse?'

Not long after that we arrived in the ramshackle settlement known as Bandit Town.

3

It was a real dump to be honest. The buildings – if you could even call them that – looked like they'd been built hastily and carelessly out of anything that had come to hand. Rusting sheets of metal had been nailed to each other, or else lashed together with jungle vines and assembled in the rough shape of little houses. Dark rubbery leaves had been ripped from the trees all around us and heaped on top of each dwelling, acting as camouflage as well as shelter, I suppose.

But the shabby buildings were the least striking thing about the small town. What stood out most was the fact that no one there was human. No one was, strictly speaking, alive. The whole town was populated by Servo-Furnishings. And each of them – whatever their size or function – was covered in the same swampy mildew and mould as the robots who had discovered us in the jungle.

'Where do you think they've come from?' Peter whispered. 'Have they escaped from the humans they're meant to look after?'

'I guess,' I said, studying them with fascination. I turned to see Toaster appraising them frankly too. His entire metal body was on the alert, bristling with keen interest. A whole town of Servo-Furnishings apparently doing their own thing in the wild… It must have been quite an eye-opener for our old sunbed.

At that same moment the 'people' of Bandit Town were getting their first look at Toaster, and you could see they were impressed. They stopped going about their business and simply stared at him. He surged forward proudly into the town square, absolutely loving the attention. Refrigerators, radiators, lamps: they all turned to gaze upon the newly restored body of Toaster. A really bizarre creation – which I later learned was a Servo in the form of an ancient gramophone player – raised its huge trumpet and gave blast of crackling noise to welcome us to their weird town. Soon there were Servo-Furnishings surrounding us on all sides as we made our way to their leader's house.

'Why they're all bandits and rogues!' I heard Toaster say, keeping his volume low. 'What a terrible-looking bunch. Cut-throats and desperadoes gone feral and wild! What will they do to us?'

Grandma hushed him. 'They're more scared of us than we are of them, believe me. Just keep your calm, Toaster.'

Finally we came to the hall of the bandit leader. We stopped and there was a hush. When he stepped out to confront us I could see that he was, in fact, a human being, though at first glance it was hard to tell. He was a portly man, wearing a golden helmet with a glass panel that distorted his face. He wore gauntlets and boots that trailed wires and tubes and a tattered scarlet cloak that gave him a kind of kinglike air, even though it was filthy and full of holes.

The leader put both gauntleted hands in the air, and the electronic buzz of robotic chatter stopped at once.

'We have guests,' he said, in a voice amplified by the helmet he wore.

Grandma stepped forward, squinting and looking less confident than a few minutes before. 'Thomas? Can it be you? Can the tales be true?'

The impassive human figure stared at her. He suddenly seemed very tall and powerful. It was obvious that every artificial being in the whole town was at his command. He could give the thumbs down right now and they could pulp us to bits in a trice. We wouldn't stand a chance.

Then the man took a step forward. In the fishbowl of his helmet his green eyes loomed and magnified as he studied us all.

His voice boomed out: 'I know you, do I?'

Grandma yelped as if she had been bit. 'Of course you do, Thomas! I'm Maggie. Maggie. Your little sister! Don't you remember me?'

Again that long, terrible pause as the large eyes behind that visor swam around, in and out of focus. The voice held no emotion whatsoever. 'Maggie?'

'It's been a long time, Thomas … many, many years … since we first arrived on this world. Sixty years or more!'

The chattering of the Servos all around us was starting up again. It was a low, whirring hum of scepticism. Who was this strange old woman, marching into town and claiming kinship with their chief? What was she playing at, making him seem so confused? The Servo-Furnishings obviously hated to see their leader confused. Maybe it was something they had never seen before.

Toaster stepped forward bravely. 'Margaret and the others are on a mission to reunite their family,' he said. 'You are part of that family, Thomas Robinson, and we need your help.'

There was a beat of silence, and then the leader removed one of his clumsy gauntlets. A pale, skinny hand started fiddling with the clasps and fastenings of his helmet. One of his favoured Servos stepped forward and raised his spindly arms to help him. And then at last the leader's mask and helmet were off. The face underneath was pale and undistinguished. It was an old man, bald as a lizard egg and struggling hard to control his tears.

'You're Maggie?' he said, and his voice wasn't booming any more. 'My little sister Maggie?'

Grandma flew into his arms. I'd never seen her move so fast. Even with her dodgy leg and her funny joints. She darted across that clearing and hugged him so hard.

Thomas was staring over her shoulder at Toaster. It was hard what to say was in that look. Amazement? Pride?

'It's okay, we're okay,' I told Peter, letting my breath out at last. The robots around us were applauding the reunion, albeit in a restrained and polite fashion.

'That's really her brother? Your uncle?' Peter asked. 'How long is it since they saw each other?'

I shrugged. 'Decades, I guess. Since their ship first crash-landed on Mars, maybe.'

Peter looked moved by the reunion. I wondered again about his own family, and whether he ever imagined meeting up with them again.

We were soon gathered up and led into the grandest building in that whole shanty town; the house belonging to their leader, my uncle Thomas.

He hugged me awkwardly and I was crushed against his clunky spacesuit, which smelled of mould.

'It's a day for rejoicing!' he cried, and the bandits all cheered. 'I am going to declare a day and a night of holiday and feasting. Yes, we'll have a feast to celebrate this wonderful meeting!' As robotic yelps of delight rang out the old man stared at me, studying my features hard. 'You're the spit of your grandma! Whoah, if that face of yours don't take me back! Maggie…! This girl's got the same danged obstinate look you always wore.'

Grandma laughed. 'I guess she does take after me a little. So – you better watch out!' She followed her brother inside the grandest of the ramshackle dwellings of Bandit Town.

'Well, if they're giving us a feast, then they must be glad to see us,' Peter reasoned.

'I suppose,' I said, still not quite sure about this strange uncle and his army of bandits.

Toaster seemed glad about our welcome, however. He was clearly delighted by the way everyone looked at him with something close to awe.

'This is how things should be done. It makes a change to get a pleasant welcome, doesn't it, Lora?'

I nodded and smiled, but he knew how I felt. I didn't really trust warm welcomes. I didn't trust any kind of welcome, these days. I knew it was best always to stay on my guard.

They served us a strange meal which we had to pretend to enjoy. We were brought slices of roasted greenish meat, which we were told came from giant grubs or caterpillars that lived in the swampland trees. I stuck to eating the bits of mushroom and deep-fried flower heads that came as side dishes. Peter and Karl ate everything they could get because they were ravenous.

Nobody in the chief's home was watching us, however. All eyes were on Grandma and her fond reunion with their leader. The two sat together on seats like thrones in the middle of the hall, locked deep in earnest conversation.

'I suppose it's like if you and Al hadn't seen each other

in sixty years,' Peter said thoughtfully, chewing on a mouthful of jellified meat.

His comment brought me up short. What if I didn't see my brother again for years? I already felt like he was lost to me. He was in the embrace of the powerful Graveley family, back in the faraway City Inside. Suddenly I saw all too clearly how families could be split up and live so far apart on a planet like Mars, and how time and the huge distances could get in the way.

I didn't want gloomy thoughts coming at me now, though. Luckily Thomas was rising to his feet to give a speech. All his Servo subjects fell silent to listen to his every word.

'Many of you here will have forgotten the tale of how we arrived in this place. New memories come to fill up the space of the old and in many cases I have had to overwrite your pasts and your previous selves in order to keep you functioning. Such is the life of the Servo-Furnishing, unfortunately, and I hope you all appreciate I have done everything I could to adapt you and to keep you alive.'

There was a mechanical buzz of agreement from the crowd that surrounded us. It wasn't just that they always obeyed their chief, I realised: every one of them completely adored him.

'Once, many years ago, longer than most of us here can remember,' he went on, 'ten Starships brought us to Mars from the blue planet Earth. We came because we wanted to, and we were great adventurers: admired by everyone on our homeworld as we went off to found a new colony here in this marvellous place. There were only a few human beings aboard this fleet of ships, but there were a great many Servo-Furnishings. A very great many of you.'

Now the Servos were responding with greater noise and enthusiastic chatter. Close to where we were standing, a fancy wooden cabinet decorated in mirrored panels was saying, 'Yes! Yes! I remember the Starships! I remember it all!'

'We came – all of us here – aboard the ship called the *Melville*. It had a rocky landing. All the ships had terrible landings on Mars. We crashed and that's why, in the first place, most of your memories were lost. The ship lost its memory, too. Its head was cracked in the hot blazing impact and all its knowledge leaked into the burning sands. And the same was true of the separate minds of many of the Servos on board, and of the humans, too – those that still lived, that is. It was a scene of hellish disaster.'

The audience members were quiet now. They were shocked at his mild tone as he described this disaster. Beside him, I saw, Grandma had tears rolling down her cheeks. She had never talked about the landing on Mars. I had always known it was calamitous, that many had died and that the colony had not started off in the way that had been planned. Times were tough. But times had always been tough for my family and I had grown up accepting this. It was strange to hear Thomas describing the very day that all our fortunes had changed forever.

'Many humans and Servos were lost. Those that survived had to scratch an existence out of the harsh and pitiless Martian prairie.'

I couldn't stop myself shouting out a question, even though everyone around me gasped at my impertinence. 'But how? How did all ten Starships crash at once? How could they? What went wrong?'

Thomas glowered at me from his throne. 'No one knows. There are stories. There are legends and theories. But mostly we don't think about that. Mars reached out and grabbed us. The planet couldn't wait for us to get here. Either that, or it tried to obliterate the lot of us before we could arrive…' He shrugged. 'It hardly matters now. It finished with most of us living a rougher life than we ever expected.'

I spoke up again. 'Grandma thought you were dead! She always talked about you as someone long gone and lost!'

Grandma gurned and grimaced at me, like I was talking out of turn, but I didn't care. I couldn't understand why she hadn't said the exact same thing. Were we supposed to act normal that he was standing here talking to us, this old guy who was supposed to have died as a boy? Grandma had mourned him for nearly sixty years. In fact, his death and that day of the crash-landing were the very things that had sent her loopy back in the first place. That was what Da always said anyway.

'Some of us chose not to live on the dusty plains of Mars,' my uncle Thomas said. 'And some of us preferred the company of loyal Servo-Furnishings to the bickering and the clamouring of other human beings. And so some of us came here, to live in the north.'

Grandma had even more tears running down her face.

Thomas stared at her. 'But you knew I was here, Maggie, surely. You knew I'd survived … didn't you?'

'T-there were rumours … and I was hoping you were alive, all that time…' she sobbed. Her voice was cracked and she didn't care that the whole room was looking at her. 'But no. I never knew you were here. Not for definite. People always assumed you were dead and gone. I can't tell you how good it is to be here. To see you again.'

'After all this time,' Thomas said. There was a strange note in his voice and I realised that he wasn't quite as pleased as Grandma was. He seemed suspicious and on his guard. 'So why are you here now, Maggie? Why did you come looking for folk you didn't even know truly existed? Why would you throw yourselves on the mercy of bandits and outcasts?'

All the electronic eyes in that room were on Grandma.

At that same moment there was a loud interruption. A wailing klaxon went off. Someone was shouting from the open main doors. 'They're here again! The skies are full of them tonight!'

Suddenly everyone was on their feet, excited, noisy, and heading for the doors.

'Who?' Peter shouted. 'What's going on?' Karl was frightened and yapping. We were almost trampled underfoot by the eager Servos.

'This night we'll be successful!' shouted Thomas. He looked gleeful, rushing to join the crowd outside. All thoughts of his new guests and what had transpired sixty years ago were seemingly forgotten. 'Tonight we'll bring one down! We will! We'll get one of them at least! I'm sure of it!'

4

'Heeeee heeeeee heeeee heeeeee!'

I knew what that noise was. Their laughter filled the night.

'Where are they? Who are they? What's going on?' Peter was shouting as the Servos went dashing about the place. Everyone was straining their eyes to see. There were swarming shapes in the night sky, blotting out the Earth light and swooping underneath the canopy of trees.

'Heeeee heeeeee heeeee!'

'It can't be! Can it? But it can't be…' I knew those hideous noises well. That sniggering: high-pitched and wavering. It was everywhere and nowhere all at once. Insidious.

Karl was yapping and baring his teeth.

I caught a glimpse of Grandma's face. She looked pale and scared in the crowd. Even with her brother beside her in all his tatty finery. He was issuing instructions and barking at his subjects.

And above us…

The skies above Bandit Town were filled with Martian Ghosts.

I'd never seen so many in all my life. In the past I had seen parties of seven or maybe even as many as ten of the creatures walking about. Dancing eerily around the place on skinny legs and silent feet. Peering in windows.

The only Martian I had ever seen properly in flight was my friend Sook. She came to me mysteriously. Suddenly we were friends and our friendship was secret. At first I didn't even realise she was the same as the creatures who were causing the Disappearances. All I knew was that Sook was my friend, and I trusted her.

She had the most beautiful moth-like wings. They were purple and chocolate-brown and they had swirling patterns on them. When I first knew her – it seems so long ago now – she would sweep me up in her arms and fly me over the deserts. I saw so much of Mars in that way, even before I left my prairie home.

Somehow I'd thought only Sook could fly.

But here, over the swamplands, soaring through the night, came a whole flock of Martian Ghosts. Their wings ruffled like silken sheets. Combined, they made a thunderous noise. And the giggling was horrible. Sinister. They weren't simply flying overhead. They were circling and looping back and peering down at the town of robot bandits.

When they came close you could pick out the spiralling lights of their eyes.

'Kill them! They'll kill us all if we don't get them first!'

All at once Thomas was frothing at the mouth and shaking both fists at the sky. His screeching made all the Servos jump up and start dashing about, as if they suddenly remembered duties they had to perform. They gathered in groups and got busy assembling little machines. I couldn't work out what they were doing at first, then it became apparent they were cannibalising each other: taking bits from this Servo, and bits from another. They were making more little machines, tapping away with wrenches and screwdrivers.

Weapons, I realised. Blasters and ray guns. Rocket launchers and bazookas. Even the most harmless-looking of the Servos were equipped with deadly attachments and now that the alarm had been sounded, out they all came. Laser flashes and bolts of sizzling energy ripped through the night air.

They weren't very good shots. Trees were set alight and soon the canopy was luminously ablaze. Some fiery missiles fell back down too soon and set light to one or two of Bandit Town's own buildings. Servos were rapidly despatched to dampen those flames.

Quite close by us several Servos were packing a short, explosive robot with horrible bombs made of impacted swamp matter and slime. Every time the squat machine exploded and fired a missile into the sky he screamed with destructive pleasure.

Toaster stared at this warlike scene and his disapproval

was etched all over his shining face. 'Oh, this is terrible,' he kept muttering to himself. 'Servos don't kill. All of this runs counter to our programming. We don't kill indigenous life forms. What are they doing, Lora? Why has their programming been perverted like this?'

I shook my head. I didn't know what to say. It was plain to me that my uncle was to blame. He had created a town where the Servo-Furnishings answered only to him and they would do anything he asked, unquestioningly. And that included shooting the Martian Ghosts out of the sky.

'They're so beautiful,' Peter said. 'I've never seen them before … not flying like this…'

Even as we watched the Martian bodies twisting in flight above us, one of those green bolts of flame fired from a bazooka met its target and hit one of the graceful if sinister creatures directly in the chest. The gorgeous wings were engulfed in flames for a few seconds and the skinny body was brightly silhouetted in its agony. Then it began to fall out of the skies, and the giggling turned to shrieks of protest and pain…

The robots cackled and chattered excitedly as the Martian fell through the branches towards the town.

'We've got one! We got one!' Thomas was croaking delightedly. I was horrified to see my grandma was hopping about, too. She looked just as excited as he did at the gruesome spectacle.

The Martian dropped out of the sky like it didn't

weigh anything at all. It fell into the middle of town on its tattered wings and all the Servos drew back and watched it.

'I don't like it here much,' Peter said quietly to me.

I had to agree.

The robots formed a ring around the fallen ghost, dancing and capering with glee. They were led in the dance by my great-uncle and my grandma.

'Leave the poor creature alone! What's the matter with you?'

I couldn't help myself. I plunged into the crowd of jostling Furnishings. I fought my way through the crowd to get to the Martian.

'Is he alive? Have you killed him? What the hell do you think you're doing?'

The robots drew back and let me through. Crazy and bloodthirsty as they were, they still knew they had to obey humans. Soon I was facing the crumpled body of the fallen creature. Its wings were frazzled black nets and its eyes were dim. There was thick, pinkish blood all over its body.

'You people are insane!' I shouted at the Servos, but really I was shouting at Thomas. 'The Martians don't mean us any harm. They never did. They were just trying to save us, the whole time…'

'Heeeee heeeee heeee…' Now the last of the Martian flock was swarming away, and the sky was drained clear of them as they fled. They knew they could do nothing for their injured friend. I was no expert, but it looked to me like it was a hopeless case.

'The Martians hate us. They taunt us! They hunt us through the swamps! They don't want us here! They never wanted us here!' Suddenly Thomas was standing opposite me. He looked like he was about to throw a fit. 'Everyone knows the Martians would kill us all if they had the chance!'

I shook my head. I knew better.

Then with what seemed to be his very last breath the Martian on the ground spoke. He looked up with those dazzling eyes as the life faded out of them and he directed his final words at me:

'We can't help you now, human child. We so wish we could. But the journey and the quest are yours. The Ancient Ones have woken up. And it is you who must go to face them, Lora Robinson. Heeee heeeeee heeeee. Only you can ... heeeee heeeeee heeeee. Only you ... heeeee heeeeee heeeee...'

As the Martian Ghost died I realised two things.

One: all those heeeee heeeeee heeeees. I always thought they were sniggering. I always thought it was hideous laughter, directed at us humans. But they were only breathing. They were struggling for breath. We coated Mars with a new atmosphere, didn't we? We reformed this world to suit ourselves. Breathing was hard for the

Martian Ghosts. At least, harder than it was for us. I figured that out as I listened to that poor guy fade away.

Two: I realised that everyone – every single inhabitant of Bandit Town – was now looking straight at me.

Thomas put their thoughts into words: 'That Martian scum knew your name, Lora Robinson. Now, tell me. How could that be so?'

I wasn't prepared right then, after everything they'd done, to tell them diddly squat. I stared back defiantly at Uncle Thomas, Grandma and all the rest.

And that's how I ended up being taken prisoner in Bandit Town and locked away for the night, even though I was such a close relation of their chief.

A single light bulb clicked and stuttered into life.

I was looking at a small lamp. It was on the other side of the bars. The lamp was looking back at me.

'Now, you won't give me any trouble, will you?' he asked nervously. His yellow filament flickered. 'It's a difficult job, watching over human beens.'

'Beings,' I told him. 'It's human beings.'

'Present tense,' he frowned. 'Makes sense. Unless you're dead, then you're a human been, aren't you? A human was?'

I was bleary and half-asleep. 'What?'

'I am Watt!' he burst out. 'Yes! I am Watt! Watt I am!' The lamp gave a little giggle, rocking the lampshade on his head, which he wore like a hat. Now I could focus a bit better, I saw that it was covered in sickly pink floral designs. My mouth fell open. Seriously? This is what they put here to guard me?

The Servo started looking nervous again. 'Y-you're not thinking of breaking out of here, are you?'

I stood up, realising that I was covered in slimy gunk from the boggy ground. A quick look at the bars told me I wouldn't be breaking out of there any time soon. 'How would I manage that?'

'I … don't know. I've met human beens before and you're tricky customers. I never know what you're capable of.' He inched closer to the bars. 'What did you do? Why did they put you in here?'

I shook my head to clear it. I could hardly remember all the details myself. The past few days ran into a confusing blur. Bandit Town. The banquet. Grandma's reunion. The swarm of Martian Ghosts and the dying man on the ground. And how he had addressed me by name.

'They think I'm a traitor, I guess,' I told the lamp. 'Because the Martian Ghost knew my name.'

Watt the lamp sucked in a shocked breath and his bulb flickered again. 'And are you a traitor? You're friends with those … those creatures? I saw them tonight, flying overhead. You know they snatch people, don't you? They make them vanish away… And some say … some have reason to believe that the Martian Ghosts *eat people*. Our chief Thomas' own wife and child were taken away once. Long ago. Or so he tells us. They were eaten by Martians!' The lamp covered up his mouth with both hands and the shade on his head was knocked awry. 'And they say that even Servo-Furnishings aren't safe. The Martian Ghosts have been known to grab us, too! And we can be Disappeared as well!'

'No, no…' I shook my head. 'It's not true, Watt. That's just how all the stories go. It's what we believed, too, back in Our Town. For years we believed that they were Disappearing us and eating us and they'd take us all away eventually and that would be the end of it. But none of that was true. My grandma Disappeared. And so did my da. But the Martians never meant us harm. They were taking us to safety. Or they thought they were.'

The lamp looked highly sceptical. 'What kind of safety? What do you mean?'

'They were taking us to the City Inside. A long way from here. But it's a city like you can't imagine. None of us could have imagined such a grand place. But that's where they thought we'd be safe. As it happens, they were wrong… No one is quite safe in the City Inside.'

The lamp shook his head. 'You're confusing me terribly. You're mixing me up. You're messing about with my thoughts. I am Watt.' He reached up and switched off his light and then clicked it back on again. 'Watt I am. And I refuse to be confused and befuddled by a human been girl.'

I shrugged. 'Whatever. But it's you lot who've got it wrong. And what you're all doing to the Martians, shooting them out of the sky and all – that's wrong, too. That's murder.'

'We are defending Bandit Town. We all have our role to play here. We are the last of our kind and we must ensure our survival.'

'You're not the last of your kind!' I said. 'Who told you that? Thomas? Well, he's wrong. There are surviving Servos all over Mars. Look at Toaster! You've seen Toaster, our friend, haven't you?'

The lamp clicked himself on and off again nervously. 'I am Watt. Watt I am. Yes, yes. I saw your Toaster. I saw the sunbed. That marvellous machine. And yet … and yet I must believe our chief and everything he says. If he is wrong about that, about this and other things … then, what if he is wrong about everything? What then? What then for Watt and Watt's kind?'

'That's what happens when you listen to just one fella,' I said. 'All you get is his version of the world. And let me tell you, Watt. As far as I can see, your Thomas – my great-uncle – he's even crazier than my grandma. And that's saying something. He's got you lot eating out of his hand and committing murder and keeping me locked up when I ought to be out and getting on with my mission…'

'Oh no! Oh no!' shrieked the lamp, clicking at his switch. 'I am Watt! I knew it! I told you, I know that human beens are slippery! They will devil me with words and other ideas! But I know right and I know wrong! There are no shades of grey. Just yes and no and right and wrong and on and off! And you are wrong, Lora Robinson. You consort with the Martian Ghosts and you've got it all quite wrong!'

'The Martians are trying to help us. They want to save us. They were warning us about the prairie. They're warning you about being here. You're too close. We were too close.'

'Too close to what?' snapped the lamp.

'To the Ancient Ones. And they're waking up, the Martians say. That man who died. The one they killed tonight. That's what he told me. The Ancient Gods underground – they're coming awake!'

'And you want me to let you out so you can run away?' asked Watt, looking scared.

'No, no,' I told him. 'I want to get out so I can *go* to the Ancient Ones. I'm actually glad they're waking up. I have to go and meet them. Face to face.'

Watt clicked his switch several times in succession. 'I am Watt! Watt I am! I shouldn't be listening to you! You're crazy! I should block you out! I should…'

FLAAASSHH!

All at once the tiny cell was flooded with searing white light.

My knight in extremely shiny armour had arrived at last.

When the X-ray lights had faded away and my sight

came back I could see that Watt the lamp was completely zonked and lying in the mud with his bulb dimmed. Looming over him was the massive shape of Toaster the sunbed.

'Lora – Bandit Town is sleeping now. It's time we were on our way.'

He reached out with his clamp-like hands and bent the solid bars of the cell quite easily. I stepped through and hugged him and paused for a while to look at the crushed form of Watt. He seemed so much smaller, lying there with his floral shade in the muck. 'Toaster, we've got to take him with us.'

'What?' Toaster said, appalled.

'Please, help me to carry him…'

Toaster was tutting, but he helped me. And together we crept out of the small jail and into the dozing, crepuscular quiet of Bandit Town by night.

5

'Who's this?' Peter wanted to know.

'Someone Lora wants to bring along,' said Toaster, and I knew he was pulling a face and raising his metal eyebrows. We were in a darkened alley at the edge of Bandit Town and we'd just met up with Peter and Karl.

I had Watt in my arms and he'd gone comatose and rigid like he'd passed out with fear.

I looked at Peter. 'You know what I'm like. Always adding new people to my gang.'

He smiled ruefully. 'I guess that's how I ended up here.'

'And aren't you glad?'

He pulled a face at that and made me laugh.

I wasn't even sure why I was insisting Watt came with us, if I was honest. It was a gut instinct, which was how – let's face it – I always decided everything.

'We must keep moving,' said Toaster.

Bandit Town was sleeping.

'It's a very curious thing,' said Toaster as he led us round the perimeter of the ramshackle dwellings. 'All the Servos sleep at the same time. Hear that electric buzzing? Like snoring. Or clockwork gradually winding down. They conserve energy together. It's like they transform back into ordinary furniture at night…'

We saw them. They looked like they were playing musical statues: all the appliances and helpful robots were frozen where they stood. But what about their chief? And Grandma?

Toaster anticipated my questions: 'I think we'll have to come back for your grandma,' he said. 'It's too dangerous to sneak into the main building and wake her now. She could raise the alarm.'

That was fine. It suited me if Grandma was happy and safe here. It allowed me to get on with the next part of our mission. She was too irascible and unpredictable to take somewhere so dangerous…

We tiptoed through the Servos' town. The slightest wrong move could trigger them to wake, Toaster warned us.

In my arms I knew Watt was conscious because his spindly arms trembled, and so did the tassles on his lampshade.

My main concern was that we get beyond the bounds of the town and back on with our quest as soon as possible. The words of the dying Martian were spurring me on. Now we knew the Ancient Ones, whoever they were, were waking. And all the Martian Ghosts – with their strangely shared minds – seemed to know I was on my way.

But which was the way? How would we know where to go?

We paused in a gloomy hollow where Toaster could activate the maps he had created of the terrain. We watched him search through charts of verdant green as images swam across the glass panels of his chest. Watt seemed to wake up at this point, and took some interest in what was going on.

He clicked his switch several times to get our attention, his warm yellow light splashing the greenish dark. 'I am Watt! If you're looking for the way into the Underworld, I know where that is.'

'You do?'

'Of course! I am Watt!' Click, click went his switch again, excitedly. 'We all know where the entrance is. We go there, quite often. That's where we take them. The tributes. The sacrifices.'

A cold dread went through me. 'Sacrifices? You mean, people?'

He nodded. 'Anyone. Anything. All the life forms that come this way. We take them to the mouth of the Underworld and whatever lives down there always seems very pleased. The Gods, they are. That's what Thomas says. He says we have to feed them and keep them happy.'

So, I thought, I should have guessed. Thomas was part of this sacrificing business, too. He was feeding folk to the Ancient Gods or whatever they were, just like Ruby was.

Peter suddenly said, 'Toaster! You've got pictures in your memory of Lora's ma and sister, haven't you? I saw them before, in the desert, when you were using that old phone's memory to make maps. You had pictures of everyone…'

Toaster was frowning and consulting his files. 'Yes, you're right.' He cleared his screen and concentrated for a moment, and then he showed us pictures of Ma and Hannah.

For a second my breath caught in my throat.

The pictures were shockingly clear and vivid. It was like the two of them were standing there before me. Ma in her bonnet and her prairie dress. She looked shabby and worn out, but my brother Al had taken the picture and caught her in a rare mood. She was laughing at him and her hair had fallen loose and wispy, so it was framing her face. She was holding my little sister in her arms and Hannah was waving both pudgy fists at Al, and her eyes were bright and they looked so happy.

It seemed like about a hundred years ago.

I couldn't even work out how long it was since we'd made our journey together. My life had stretched out of all shape since then. My heart leapt up inside me with hope and fear as I remembered what we had come all this way to do.

They had to be alive. And we just had to find them.

'I've seen these human has-beens!' cried Watt the lamp. His voice was shrill and excited. 'The mother and the girl! Of course, I know them! I am Watt! I talked with them. I watched over them when they were here!' He clicked his switch madly.

I seized him in my arms. 'You know them?'

'Watt I am! Ages ago. So long ago. Weeks and months ago. I don't know. My sense of time is erratic, I'm afraid. It's to do with clicking myself on and off, you see. I have no idea of time passing when my switch is off. But yes! I know them.' Then a sadness seemed to settle over him. 'I can take you to the entrance of the Underworld. It's where we took them. It's where we sent them. They were taken underground to the Gods. And the Sentinels came to fetch them. Of course, but you knew that, didn't you?'

'Yes, we knew that already,' I said. 'It's how come we're here. We're going to bring them back.'

Watt looked amazed. 'No one comes out of there again. They never have, you know.'

'This will be a first,' I said grimly. 'Come on. Let's keep moving before Bandit Town wakes up. You're gonna show us the way, little Watt.'

'I will,' he said. 'I was never happy sending prisoners down there. I always got to know them, you see, sitting with them in the jail. It always seemed such a shame... But, quickly. We must be on our way. Thomas will be furious when he realises we have gone. It will serve him right, but he's got a nasty temper ... I've seen him do terrible things to Servos...'

'Come along,' Toaster urged, getting up and leading the way deeper into the trees.

So, though I hadn't planned it at all, there was method in my madness. I had grabbed Watt and brought him along on our quest and the others had thought I was crazy, but it was Watt who led us to the entrance to the Underworld.

We sloshed and slogged through several miles of boggy groves, ducking through curtains of vine and creeper until at last we came to a certain obscure corner. Somewhere we'd probably never have noticed if we'd come this way by ourselves. There was a green hummock in a soggy glade, sheltered by ancient trees and there, hidden by rushes and furry grasses, was a dark portal.

'This is this place!' shouted the lamp excitedly. 'This is where they get brought. The sacrifices! They stand there and we stand here. All the Servos who can light up stand here in a row, shining the way into this doorway.'

It looked a pretty nasty doorway. There was nothing grand or spectacular about it, heralding the entrance to a new world where the Gods all dwelled. It was slimy and horrible and there wasn't even a door to open.

'They sent Ma and Hannah this way?'

Watt nodded sadly. 'There was nothing I could do. I am only Watt.'

I tried picturing my ma and my sister venturing through that dark doorway. They must have been terrified. Hannah was still too young to understand properly, perhaps. But she was older now, wasn't she? Kids grow up fast. Perhaps she understood all too well she was being sent somewhere strange and dangerous…

Ma would have been grim and resigned. She would have been defiant to the last.

'How long ago, Watt?' Peter asked. 'How long is it since your chief sent them down this way?'

Watt frowned and his bulb dimmed with the effort. 'Months. Not days, not weeks. It's more like months.' He looked at me sadly. 'I'm sorry, Lora. It might be too late for them.'

Toaster stepped forward then, pushing out his glass chest unit as if he was plucking up his courage. 'But we don't know anything for sure, do we? We don't know what exactly lives down there in the Underworld. No one does, really. We don't know what or who they have met. There's no point in bellyaching and worrying above ground. All we can do is follow in their footsteps.'

Peter nodded. 'Toaster's right.'

'You don't have to come along as well, Peter,' I told him. 'You and Karl have come far enough for my sake. Maybe you could stay here. Build a little camp for when we come back out. Wait here for us.'

'Nuh-huh,' he said. 'I'm not waiting anywhere. We've come this far with you. Just look at everything we've been through. We've been arrested and locked up and we've escaped and crash-landed! We've travelled halfway across Mars together!' Karl was barking joyfully at Peter's words, sharing his enthusiasm and determination. 'Do you really think we'd let you go on by yourself? With just a table lamp and a sunbed for company?'

Both Servos looked slightly miffed by this, but I knew what Peter meant. It was true we'd come a long way together. I pictured him as I first saw him, wearing his ragged red jumper and busking in the market underneath the building where I used to live in the City Inside. It all seemed a lifetime ago but in reality it was just a few short months.

Suddenly Toaster was looking alarmed. 'My sensors detect life forms and servo-energy signatures in the vicinity, Lora.'

'Meaning that my uncle and my grandma are coming after us?'

'They're twenty minutes behind us, at the most.'

Dawn was coming, through the dense swamplands. We couldn't quite get a proper view of the skies as they turned pinkish-gold, but enough of those colours came streaking through the rubbery canopy leaves to let us know that night was over. The swamp was stirring with waking life all around us. As the murky air turned brighter Watt switched off his bulb in order to conserve energy. 'I reckon I'll need it in the Underworld,' he said bravely. 'I am Watt. My job is to illumine the way.'

'You really don't need to come any further, Watt,' Peter told him. 'You could stay here and tell the others we kidnapped you. Forced you to bring us here against your will.'

Watt was firm. 'I am Watt. I light the way. I'm here to help you.'

And that was all he had to say on the matter.

By now I could hear noise emanating from the thickest, darkest part of the jungle. Clanking, robot noises of vegetation being cleared for humans. The rumbling noise of all the Servos of Bandit Town hot on our heels. It was clear that they were catching us up.

'Okay. We'd best go. Do you think they'll come after us? Down there?'

Watt was brushing dried mud and slime off his lampshade. 'Oh no. Not Thomas. He has a dread of the Underworld. But he might send Servos after us. It all depends. If he wants you back, Lora. Then he might send folk to fetch you.'

Then the little Servo lamp shot ahead of us all, splashing through the shallow pools to the unassuming entrance of the Underworld. He stepped into the darkness and clicked his light back on. 'I am Watt. Follow me!'

And we set off in a line, with the reassuring bulk of Toaster bringing up the rear.

'It's a little bit tight,' the sunbed said, squeezing himself through the entrance. 'I hope it's not going to be a very claustrophobic kind of Underworld...'

None of us knew what kind of Underworld it might turn out to be. All we knew so far was darkness and damp and a tingling warmth in the air.

6

The walls on either side of us as we went down and down and down were covered in writing, scratched into the dry, red rock. Hyro-griffics, is what they were called, according to Toaster. They were extremely old. In fact, even he couldn't tell how old they were or what language they were in: that's how far they went back. He didn't have a single clue what they were saying.

'Someone must have spent their lifetime carving these,' said Peter. His face was lit up with wonder, moving from one set of carvings to the next. He looked like he wanted to stop and puzzle them out.

Watt was in his arms, lighting up patches of the blood-red walls. When I looked closer I could see there were little pictures, too, amongst the scratchy writing. Symbols representing things: little creatures, maybe. Animals like I've never seen.

We'd been travelling down into the tunnel maybe three hours by then. Toaster and Watt took turns leading the way with their lights shining in the gloom, trying to conserve their energy and now Toaster's luminous chest was in front. He marched determinedly down the sandy staircase, insisting that we shouldn't spend too long examining these amazing walls.

'I get the feeling not many humans have seen these hyro-griffics,' I mused. 'Shouldn't we … take pictures of them? Keep a record of them?'

Toaster seemed dismissive. 'That's what Dean Swiftnick of the university would have done,' he said. 'He'd have forced me to photograph every inch of these walls. I'd be stuck here forever, making a historical record! And then where would we be?'

'He's right,' said Peter. 'We could spend our lives gawping at this stuff. But we have to get on, don't we?'

I guess I was starved of words and pictures. That's what it was. I'd been on the move and having adventures for so long. Something inside me was craving the idea of sitting still for once.

There must have been so many secrets on these walls, deep under the surface of our world.

'How much deeper do you think we'll have to go?' Peter asked. 'I just realised that we haven't brought any food or water with us.'

I looked at him sharply. He was right. How come I hadn't thought of that?

'We're just traipsing merrily into the Underworld,' he said, 'with absolutely nothing to keep us alive.'

'More of my great planning,' I joked. But neither of us laughed.

Toaster was listening for signs of life. His newly restored instruments were stretched to their fullest capacity, straining into the darkness and the depths, hoping to hear something that signalled life.

'It's all very confusing,' he said. 'Because there *are* signs. But nothing that is familiar. It's an alien kind of life compared to what we know. The signs are quite different.'

'Keep trying,' I told him.

Then he looked worried. 'Also, I believe, we are still being followed.'

'Uncle Thomas?'

The sunbed nodded. 'And your grandmother, with Servos to help them. They are pursuing us after all.'

I couldn't hear anything coming down the tunnel behind us. Had we come so far already?

'I can't hear anything. It's quiet here,' I said.

'Your ears are full of noisy interference, that's why,' said Toaster.

Silence. Then: a low-pitched buzz was filling the air. It was almost too low for humans to detect, but it was there. It was a slow, throbbing beat, from deep below us. It blocked out any other sounds we might have heard.

'What is it?' Peter asked.

'I think it's our destination,' said Toaster mysteriously.

Knowing that Thomas and his motley crew were on our tails spurred me on. I wasn't prepared to hang around trying to read hyro-griffs with them coming up behind and spoiling our mission. We carried on and I tried to concentrate on that heartbeat. It was in my chest, vibrating in all my bones and coming up through my tired, aching feet.

We walked for hours on end, with the walls pressing closer and the ground getting steeper. The panicky thought kept coming to me: what if there was no end to this? What if we just kept walking and walking and it was forever downwards? What if there never was an end to it?

Those are just the tricks your mind plays on you, of course. I should have known that by now. And I should have known that, as soon as you start thinking like that, something – some unknown thing – turns out to be just around the corner.

All of a sudden there was a group of three small creatures before us in the cramped tunnel. They stood no higher than my waist.

'Sentinels,' Watt said, clicking his light worriedly.

They were smooth-skinned, luminous and blue, with rounded snouts and small dark eyes.

We drew back from them in fright, but they seemed to mean us no harm. One of them started talking to us in a low, burbling voice, but it was hard to make out his words. Then all three were surrounding us, pulling at our sleeves and at Toaster's bulky metal limbs.

We followed them down the tunnel and came at last to a vast, underground hollow. There was a strange luminosity that seemed to come out of the very walls and from the ancient-looking tall, gnarled tree in the centre of the cave. Its many thousands of leaves were pale and glowing.

'How can there be a tree growing all the way down here?' Peter asked.

I didn't know. All I knew was that it made me feel strange, just looking at it, and the way those leaves shivered, even though there was no breeze in the cavern.

Then I realised there was a human figure standing in front of the tree. She was the largest woman I had ever seen.

'Who's that?' Peter said, grasping my arm.

The woman threw out her arms and roared with welcoming laughter.

'Whoever she is, she seems glad we've landed up on her doorstep!'

She was dressed in layers of brightly coloured fabrics. As we drew closer we could see that there were leaves woven into her clothes, too. Her face was one huge gap-toothed grin and her eyes were squinched almost shut.

'Welcome, welcome, come on in!' She ushered us along and her little Sentinel helpers were pushing us towards the staircase carved into the trunk of that gigantic tree.

The steps spiralled up and up into the branches and at first Toaster protested that they would never bear his weight. 'Ha! But look at me!' laughed the enormous woman. 'Just look at the size of me! They hold me up every day, don't they?' She threw back her huge, shaggy head and laughed.

Peter and I exchanged glances, and Karl whined worryingly. Who was this old, gargantuan person? Why were we just letting her boss us about?

'Ah, you mustn't be shy of me,' she shouted at us. 'I know I'm strange and noisy and all the rest of it, but I mean well. I know what you've come this way for, and I'm keen to help you.'

I frowned. 'You know why we've come?'

She pushed her grizzled face close to mine. Her teeth were rotting stumps and her breath smelled of something sweet, like she'd been chewing on herbs from the swamps. 'Surprises you, does it? Ha! Well, Ma Taproot knows stuff. I'm like the tree, you see. The roots go very far and wide into the mud and I pick up whispers and clues and little secrets, you see? And I know all kinds of surprising things. Now, come along! I know that you lot are completely starved after your days running through deserts and swamps and tunnels and all…'

As she led the way up the carved steps she was moaning and sighing like any old lady might about her ancient joints, yet she seemed pretty sprightly to me.

Toaster was looking very disturbed. 'I found no trace of this person or this tree in my scans,' he told me. 'She managed to cloak herself somehow from my sensors.'

Ahead, the person who called herself Ma Taproot let

out a shout of laughter and called back, 'Oh, Toaster! You do make me laugh! And I'm so pleased to meet you in person. You're just as fussy and silly as I knew you'd be!'

Toaster was starting to look pretty annoyed. He hissed at me: 'How could she know anything about us?'

The small lamp was struggling with the steps – they were too widely spaced for him – so I had to carry him again. 'I am Watt!' he gabbled. 'And I have heard tell of this vast and mysterious female person, who lives in the ground in the Underworld. There are stories about her in the northern lands! She is a legend to the Servos of Bandit Town and beyond!'

'Well, I've never heard of this person,' said Toaster huffily. 'To be honest, she seems rather vulgar and untrustworthy to me.'

Ma Taproot gave another bark of laughter. Then we reached her home.

The doorway was before us, wide open in welcome. She lived in a generously sized space right inside the tree trunk. It was easily as large as the hall my uncle Thomas lived in, but it was far cosier. After all our travels and living rough, our makeshift camps and the discomforts of places like Ruby's town, this was absolute luxury. The furniture was beautiful and old-fashioned, plump and soft and gorgeously colourful. Ma Taproot certainly enjoyed being comfortable.

'Please, make yourselves at home,' she urged us, and

clapped her massive hands at her small helpers. 'These people need refreshments!'

Peter looked so relieved he could almost cry. 'I thought we were going to be climbing down and down those steps forever,' he said. 'And we hadn't even brought any water or nothing.'

I felt a bit like he was having a dig at me, as leader of our expedition. Like I had been remiss in the plan-making department. I was about to snap at him, when I realised Ma Taproot was watching us carefully. 'Then you are fortunate to fall into my hands,' she told us. 'I can give you nectar and honey and manna from heaven. I can give you all the best things to eat and drink. I could even give you your hearts' desires. It's true. You're very lucky. And I am very lucky, too, to meet you people at last.'

In the softly flickering light it was possible to get a good look at her now. She seemed hardly human. Troll-like, really, with her massive shoulders and her boulder-like head and ropes of hair. Her clothes were rags and leaves. She looked just like a huge mound of laundry, piled up any old how. But her words were kind. Her voice had turned quieter and softer. She sounded concerned for us.

'You know who we are?' Peter asked. 'How could you know anything about us?'

She chuckled. 'Ma Taproot can feel out the truth, like I told you. My limbs and my roots extend in all directions. For example, Peter, I know that your home for several years has been under the ground, same as mine. But a long, long way from here. You live underneath the magical City, don't you? Secretly. Hiding yourself away with others. Such a pity. But, you see? I know a little about you. And your dearest pet, whom you almost lost, once.' She smiled and went to pat Karl's head. He snapped at her. 'Ah, you mustn't be scared of old Ma Taproot.'

Peter had turned pale. No one knew his secrets. Or not many people. How could this woman, all this distance away, know anything about us?

'And you're Lora Robinson,' said the old woman, turning those dark eyes on me. They were brown and gold. They flickered with a deep internal flame. 'I know your name. I know your tale.'

'D-do you?' I said, toughing it out. I tried to look like it meant nothing to me, whatever she knew. What did I care that everyone on this strange journey seemed to know my name? 'I suppose your roots and branches told you all about me as well?' I tried to sound mocking.

'Well, yes,' said Ma Taproot. 'Naturally. But something else told me all about you, Lora, and your various adventures and your quest. Or should I say: someone.'

Straight away I was suspicious. She was toying with me. She was going to tell me something terrible now. We had placed ourselves at her mercy and now she was about to reveal that we were in danger...

'Who? Who could have told you anything about me?'

65

'Ah,' she sighed. 'Who do you think?'

My heart started to race. 'Ma! You've seen my ma and my sister Hannah. Have they been here? Have they been this way?'

She stared deeply into my eyes and sighed. 'I'm sorry, Lora. But I never talked to your mother or your sister. I know how much you want to know what's been happening to them. But I'm afraid I must tell you I haven't spoken with them.'

'But you've seen them?' I shot back. My pulse was racing.

'Oh, yes. I caught a glimpse of them as they passed through my realm. They were well. They are safe, Lora.'

I stared at her, feeling a huge swell of relief. 'But … where are they? Can we find them?'

The old lady chuckled. 'You mustn't race important tasks. These things must be done in the right order.'

My eyes were on her as she swept around her cosy living space. I cast a glance at Peter and he frowned. Was this strange old woman playing games with us? She had all this knowledge, and she seemed to know about Ma. I had to keep her friendly…

'Aren't you interested to know who told me all about you, Lora Robinson?' Ma Taproot leaned close, treating me to a huge grin.

'Yes,' I said. 'Please, tell me.'

'Sook,' she said simply. 'Your friend Sook has told me all about you.'

7

You know when someone blurts something out that you're just not expecting? And your head goes into a whirl? That's how I was just then, when Ma Taproot told me about Sook.

'When did you see her?' I gasped. 'How long ago?'

Ma Taproot laughed, settling back into her comfortable chair. 'Time moves differently down here. It might have been last week, or it might have been many years ago...'

'Please, try to think,' I begged. 'I don't know if Sook is safe. I haven't seen her since we were in the City. I've heard her voice in my head, but I don't know if that was me imagining things or not...'

I realised that my friends Peter and Toaster were looking at me strangely by now. They didn't know much about Sook, the Martian Ghost. I had said very little about her, and they respected that. For a long time I had been worried about her. Ever since I had last seen her, just after Christmas, when she came to Da's flat and told me that she had been a prisoner of the Authorities. They had trapped her in a killing jar and glued her wings together. She had escaped to come and see me, even though her wings were damaged and tattered. Those beautifully coloured, butterfly wings.

'I need to know that she's alive and safe,' I said, more calmly now. 'The Authorities weren't happy with her.'

'The City-dwellers hate anyone who doesn't live exactly as they do,' Ma Taproot sighed. 'I have seen many Martian Ghosts, Lora. They venture into these wild parts of the world quite frequently. Even though it is dangerous to them. They come here and plead with me and tell me I must leave this place and my home in the tree. It isn't safe here because it is too close to the Ancient Ones and the Heart of Mars. Sook tried to warn me of such things, too.' She chuckled.

'We've been told the same,' Peter burst out. 'That's where we're going! And the Ancient Ones are waking up, we've heard. We're going to talk with them. Is it … is it really that dangerous?'

Ma Taproot let out one of her huge guffaws of laughter and slapped her massive knees. 'This boyfriend of yours, Lora. Has he no guile? Has he no common sense? He just comes out with it – easy as anything! Telling me all! Revealing your quest! Aren't you suspicious, boy? Don't you think you should be more careful?'

Peter blushed deeply and looked away. 'I suppose I should … I just … I just reckoned I could trust you. I felt that I could.'

The old woman snorted. 'Perhaps you can and perhaps

you can't. But it's best not to go blurting out your plans to strangers. You need to hush your boyfriend, Lora.'

I squirmed, wanting to get back to the subject of Sook. 'He's not my boyfriend.'

'Well, I know that's the truth,' nodded Ma Taproot. 'I know that it's a boyfriend of his own he's looking for. One day, maybe, when things are settled and you can stop having adventures. One day, maybe.'

'Please,' I broke in. 'Ma Taproot, think hard. Think about Sook. When did you last see her? And were her wings still damaged?'

'Now that you come to mention it, I think maybe they were. She had worn herself out, flying all the way to the north. She was exhausted and slept here. And her wings were almost ruined, you're right. My heart went out to her. She was searching for her father, she said. She had lost his heartbeat in her own heart. She could find no trace of him anymore…'

'Oh,' said Peter, and exchanged a glance with me. We both knew what had become of Sook's da. It was a weird coincidence, and a horrible moment we had shared. He was a prisoner back in the town where Ruby ruled. They had lassoed him down out of the sky and broken his wings, convinced he was going to attack them. We had found him when he was dying and realised who he was. I had bad news to give when I next saw Sook.

'We met her father,' I told the old woman. 'And he told

us more about what the Martian Ghosts were up to, and how they were friends to us human settlers in more ways than we'll ever know. They were warning us. They were trying to save us. They were telling us to keep away from this whole country. To steer clear of the Ancient Ones.'

'That's right,' Ma Taproot nodded. 'The Martian Ghosts, as you people call them, were only trying to do right by you.'

Toaster's electronic voice broke in then, almost rudely. 'And you, Mrs Taproot. Are you a human being? What manner of creature are you?'

She eyed him carefully and grunted. 'I'm being asked to define myself by a walking, talking sunbed? Ha! What do you care what manner of being I am? Am I human? Am I Martian? Maybe I hail from the planet Venus! What business is it of yours, huh? What do you care what my role is here? I'm Ma Taproot! I'm mother to everyone here. I'm the one who holds it all together. It's only me who can keep it all under control, you know. You should be a polite guest, Mr Toaster, and keep your personal questions to yourself.'

She clapped her huge hands together grandly, and more of those blunt-nosed, black-eyed Sentinel creatures came running to do her bidding.

'Please, it's late,' she said. 'Let my guests retire and bathe and replenish themselves with sleep. Ma Taproot grows weary, and so must they, too. They have come so very far to be with her.'

I found it almost impossible to believe that all those rooms could fit inside her tree. Soon I was disoriented, as I followed the stumpy Sentinel creatures to a room of my own. From the tiny window I had a view of pale branches and those eerie white leaves, trembling in the dark.

I was so exhausted I didn't mind being separated from the others. The wine and food we had been given made me feel sleepy and satisfied. I was filled with a glow that I hope meant I was safe, and not just drugged. No, I was pretty sure we could trust Ma Taproot.

The strange creatures led me to a glorious bathroom with a deep golden tub, filled with pink bubbles. They pointed out pyjamas and a multi-coloured robe for me to put on afterwards. The bedroom they showed me to was ridiculously opulent and gorgeous. The glittering chandelier put me in mind of stuff I'd seen in the Graveley apartment in the City: and they were the richest folk I had ever met.

As I took my late-night bath I wondered vaguely how Toaster and Peter were getting on. And Watt. Something about that odd little lamp tugged at my heart.

Once I was in my pyjamas and alone in that wonderful room, there was a light tap at the door.

'Peter? What's up?'

He was wearing similar pyjamas and his hair was mussed up and half-wet. He looked worried.

'Come and see this,' he said, and I followed him without thinking.

71

We took the spiral staircase back down through the tree house. I had just about lost my bearings completely, but Peter seemed to know where we were heading.

'It's her, she's talking to Toaster,' he explained in a breathy kind of voice. 'I thought you'd want to hear this…'

Soon we were back in Ma Taproot's cosy sitting room. She was still there, but now she was in some kind of huge nightgown, lacy and cream-coloured. The gown made her features look even coarser, and her hands even more gnarled.

She was surrounded by her Sentinels and their dark eyes were intent upon Toaster, who was glowing. They clustered about him and all at once they seemed sinister to me, with their dark, clever eyes.

I gasped because his electronic eyes had gone back into his head and he seemed to be floating off the wooden floor somehow.

'I would like to hear more of your secrets, please, Toaster,' said the old woman softly, gruffly. 'I can't sit up all night waiting.'

Toaster seemed to be wrestling with himself, and resisting her.

I tried to spring forward, but Peter held me back. 'No, don't,' he whispered.

'You're very important, Toaster, I know that,' said Ma Taproot, in a low and calculating voice. 'You were there at the start of this story and I have a feeling you'll be there at the end. Please tell me what you're hiding.'

My blood was running cold. So she *was* a monster, after all. Interrogating our friend like this! She was a villain, just like all the rest.

'Please, please let him go free,' cried a shrill voice, and it took me a moment to realise that it was our lampstand friend standing there.

'I am Watt! I have no secrets to speak of and I'm pretty boring, but please let me stand in Toaster's place! Why don't you take me? Drain my mind instead!'

Ma Taproot laughed gurglingly at Watt, and swiped him aside with one lumpy foot. Again I tried to burst forward, but Peter stopped me. I could hear growling somewhere near the ground, and realised that Karl was with us, too.

What was the old woman doing to Toaster?

He started talking. Haltingly. At first, as if every word was being dragged out of him. Then with more ease, as the memories came flooding back into his robot mind.

'Yes, I have secrets and … I was there at the start, as you say, Ma Taproot. But there are many beginnings, and the start of one story might be the ending of many others, and the ending of…'

'Enough,' she interrupted. 'Flim flam. Get on with it. Tell me when you first came into the tale.'

'I … I saw them when they were children. Margaret Estelle Robinson and Ruby, who was the daughter of a captain of one of the ten fabled Starships from Earth. And also, Margaret's fine brother, Thomas.

'They lived in a hotel that final month on Earth, near the spaceport where the ten Starships were waiting to be launched and flung into the skies in the direction of Mars. The rain lashed down all that month. The whole country was awash and there were hurricanes and cyclones and flooding and there were even concerns that the Starships would never be launched. But the engineers and the pilots laughed at this: never had such ships been built before. Nothing could stop them venturing forth on their quest.'

Peter and I turned to look at each other. This was ancient stuff. Toaster was talking about memories of more than sixty years ago. Memories of Earth. We held our breath and silently urged him on. We wanted to know more, just as Ma Taproot did.

'Go on, Toaster,' the old woman said in her crumbly voice. 'Where were you? *What* were you back then?'

His shoulders seemed to shrug and his head sunk down into his shoulders. 'I wasn't even a sunbed in those days. I was nothing. But I had ambition! I had ideas! I had heard all about this mission and the ten Starships and the chosen few who were going to be travelling to Mars.

'They were all staying in the hotels in the spaceport. I managed to get myself on to the staff of the fanciest hotel. I was nothing but a menial Servo. A window cleaner for this five-hundred-storey glass tower.

'I had six suckered legs and I had to climb up the outside of the hotel, squooshing all the windows and wiping them down. Completely pointless in the rain, of course. But I was on a mission. And I found them.

'I found Margaret and Ruby and Thomas, and the suite they had to themselves. They were waiting for their year's journey through space to begin and they were impatient and bored. I tapped on their window, and they let me in…'

'So you won their confidence. You inveigled your way into their company,' mused Ma Taproot.

'I won their friendship!' Toaster protested. 'I had a strong feeling as soon as I met those kids that we were destined to be great friends. Margaret, especially, thought I was amazing. I was just a lowly window cleaner. I was a kronky little robot who had seen better days.

'But I told them I had dreamed about travelling through the stars and the endless void of space. I confessed all the dreams that plagued me when I was supposed to be shut down and recharging myself.

'They could hardly believe that a simple machine such as myself could have these powerful feelings and dreams…'

'Yes,' said Ma Taproot. 'It's one of the miracles of life, isn't it? The way feelings gather inside of you. Whoever you are. Under the surface. The feelings can build up and long for true expression. Even inside the most unlikely of beings. The most impossible of creatures. Even a Servo.'

'Especially a Servo!' Toaster snapped at her crossly. 'What had I ever done with my life? Where had I been?

All I had ever done was serve human beings. And not even indoors. All my jobs so far had been cleaning windows, cutting grass, polishing the concrete and steel exteriors of lofty buildings. It was a terrible life. And I always knew I was cut out for more!'

'They decided to take you with them,' Ma Taproot prompted. 'They found you a space aboard their Starship.'

'Space was at a premium. Every ounce and every pound and every square inch was accounted for. How could they have smuggled me in? They would have been in ghastly trouble. But luckily the girls decided to confide in Thomas. He was a Servo expert, young as he was. He was obsessed with my kind. And he was intrigued by my single-mindedness. My determination. My pleasingly singular personality.'

'Don't grow boastful, Toaster,' Ma Taproot chuckled. 'So, in short, he promised to get you aboard their ship?'

'The *Melville*,' said Toaster. 'He recognised, same as I did, that my destiny lay among the stars, and on the planet Mars. And so he took my robot brain out of my body and, in a delicate and dangerous operation, he put it here. Inside this sunbed. And the sunbed had a place aboard the *Melville*, of course. It was a very luxurious vessel. I was to be the personal sunbed to the Robinsons, but also their advisor and their protector.'

'You must have been very proud of yourself.'

'I was! And I am! For I am still here, fulfilling that role.'

'And your destiny is still awaiting you,' said Ma Taproot. 'There are still many important tasks for you to fulfil.'

All at once the strange glow around Toaster faded away and he settled gently back down on the ground.

His lamp-like eyes came back into focus and he blinked slowly, as if emerging from a trance. 'I … I feel like I have said too much. I have given too much away.'

'On the contrary,' smiled Ma Taproot. 'I am custodian of so many stories. Vital stories. The stories of some of the most important happenings that Mars has ever witnessed. Your testimony tonight will join those tales. Thank you.'

I could have sworn that Toaster was preening himself at her words. 'Important tales, eh? Well, I'm nothing but a servant, really. I have just done what was asked of me.'

'I think you're a very important person indeed,' said the old woman, clambering down from her chair. 'A very useful person, perhaps.' And then she was lumbering off, without another word, towards her own bedroom.

Watt was standing in his small golden glow, staring up at Toaster with hero worship in his eyes. 'I am Watt,' Watt said.

'I know,' sighed Toaster. 'What do you want?'

'I was on one of the Starships, too, all those years ago. But I remember hardly anything. I think it was the *Emily Dickinson*. But I was nothing. A reading lamp in the second-class lounge. I never saw anything interesting happen at all. But you, Toaster … you and your story … why, you are legendary!'

By now the room had cleared of Ma Taproot's helpful Sentinels, and I felt free to emerge from our hiding place by the door. 'Oh, please. Don't give him any more of a swollen head than he's already got!'

Toaster looked down at me and Peter solemnly. 'Lora! You were listening in?'

'Couldn't help it,' I said. 'And fascinating it was, too.'

'I … I couldn't control my mouth. It was the old woman. Something about her got inside my circuits. The way she talks … it was like she had turned my thoughts to liquid and she was pouring them all out of me. The tale I told … I could hardly recall the details inside my own mind, but once I started talking…'

I was looking up into his old, familiar face. 'I think she's right, Toaster. But I've always thought there's something special about you. I knew it.'

'Thank you,' he said.

'Just don't get boastful,' I warned.

Then Karl was barking and Peter, I realised, was over by one of the windows. He was peering out through the pale leaves into the subterranean night. 'Oh no,' he said, and the awful tone of his voice immediately put me on my guard.

'What is it?'

'Can't you hear that?' He fiddled with the catch and pushed the window open. All I could hear at first was the gentle shushing motion of the branches and those leaves. 'Listen,' he said.

Then I could hear them. Their voices and hallooing cries were horribly distorted by the underground tunnels.

'The Servos from Bandit Town,' Peter said. 'They've come after us.'

8

They thought they were rescuing us, they said.

Uncle Thomas had an almost superstitious dread of the dangers that lurked underground. He had heard terrible things about Ma Taproot. He'd wasted no time in telling Grandma every awful rumour he had ever heard. She was a monster who ate human brains to keep herself alive. She ate anything she could get her hands on: even Servo-Furnishings. She would crunch up bones and steel and polished wood between her teeth, which she kept sharpened, like knives.

So, in a way, it was brave of them to launch a rescue mission for us. It could be seen as courageous, that they came charging down the tunnels, whooping and hollering in the middle of that night. Peter was more sceptical than I was. He said it was all for badness and mischief. He hadn't liked the look of Thomas from the start. He thought he was all kinds of crazy.

There was a terrific racket as the Servos emerged from the tunnel into the cavern where Ma Taproot lived. For a moment or two the party stopped in their mechanical tracks and simply stared at the ghostly, gigantic tree.

To them Ma and her home were a legend. No one they knew had ever come as far as this place and been allowed to return. They all stood there staring.

What a ramshackle bunch they made. Away from their habitat of the swamps and Bandit Town, they looked even odder. Once smooth and precision-engineered, these mobile machines with their telescopic arms and electronic eyes now looked shabby and broken down. They were scabbed with bloody rust and blanketed in foul-smelling mildew and moss.

'Half of Bandit Town has come after us,' Peter gasped, when we got a clear view of them, emerging from the tunnel.

'They've got great timing,' I muttered, and watched as Toaster swept into action, making for the door. 'Toaster, wait! What are you doing?'

'We can't allow them to attack,' he said. 'Ma Taproot and her people aren't our enemies. Nor are they enemies of the Servos.'

He hurried towards the exit and I realised he was right. We didn't know much about Ma Taproot and her motives yet, but we sure didn't need rescuing by mob-handed Servos.

'Come on,' I told Peter and Karl, and we dashed after Toaster to the wooden staircase that spiralled round the tree.

All around us there was frenetic activity, as the small

servants of Ma Taproot swept into action. There was no denying the Sentinels' grim efficiency and determination. They might be small and innocuous-looking, but they understood at once that their mistress' home was under attack and that it was their duty to defend it.

'There's going to be a battle,' said Peter. 'How can we stop them?'

Suddenly it seemed like everything was happening all at once. No sooner had I got a glimpse of Uncle Thomas and Grandma in the crowd, than it seemed that a ruckus had broken out. There was a series of brilliant flares set off from the tree itself, which lit up the interior of the cavern in shocking bursts of azure blue and pink. There was so much sudden noise the attacking Servos howled with dismay.

'These are just warning shots,' Toaster mused. 'Harmless. They're trying to scare them away.'

All over the tree Ma Taproot's servants were dashing about. Their stumpy arms worked busily at launching more of those balls of light and noise. Fireworks, they were, I guess. So that was something. At least they were relatively harmless. But imagine fireworks set off in the close confines of subterranean tunnels. Each time they crackled and spat their brilliant colours we all went deaf and a bit blind.

The Servos were disorientated and they were shouting angrily into the chaotic darkness. All at once they seemed like a hopeless bunch. They were just junk. Old, rubbishy junk that had managed to stay alive for years in the swamplands.

There were perhaps as many as thirty robots down there, all of them going crazy with their myriad sensors in disarray.

'There's your uncle,' said Peter, nudging me. 'Look, can't we go down and tell him to back off? What on Mars are they doing coming down here?'

We got the answer to that a couple of moments later. During a pause in the fireworks there came a crackling and a booming from an electronic loudspeaker. Someone had put a megaphone into the hands of my grandma and her voice came hollering up to where we stood.

'Cease and desist this bombardment! We come in peace! We have come to beg you for the lives of my young granddaughter and her friends!'

'What?' Peter laughed. 'Boy, has your grandma got it wrong again!'

Her voice rang out once more: 'Please, please let her go free! Lora has had such an unfortunate life so far. Please, please don't eat her!'

Now I could see Grandma, in the middle of that crowd of bewildered Servos. She was holding a great big funnel-thing to her mouth and yelling into it, looking like she was on the verge of tears. Beside her was a robot who was made out of loudspeakers: every bit of him was vibrating as she squawked out each word. I'd grown up hearing my crazy grandma yelling. To me, this was like a mortifying nightmare.

'I'd better go down there and explain to her…' I said. 'Grandma was always getting the wrong end of the stick.'

'No,' said a gruff voice behind me. 'Let me go down and talk to them.'

Ma Taproot was emerging from her home, bundled up in a huge dressing robe made of some kind of patchwork material. She had a rug over her shoulders and a heavy scarf over her wild and twiggy hair.

'Ma Taproot, I'm sorry,' I said. 'It's my grandma … she's brought these Servos here, looking for me…!'

Ma Taproot looked haggard: the lines in her face like a chart of the canals and craggy contours of our world itself.

She clicked her fingers and commanded her creatures to stop letting off fireworks and several moments later our ears stopped ringing.

She lumbered heavily down the spiral stairs and we followed in her wake.

Grandma yelled: 'I've been told all about you, the cannibal woman who lives underground! She'll eat anything! To see her is to court a horrible death! My brother Thomas has told me the tales about you.'

'Has he indeed?' Ma Taproot shouted back in her voice that was as deep as the tunnels beneath our feet. 'Well, if I'm so scary, what brings you down here? Why are you tempting fate by waking an old, hungry woman up in the middle of the night?'

'Because you've got Lora, that's why!' Grandma bellowed. 'And you mustn't harm that girl! She's got important things to do. She is on a quest!'

'Is that a fact?' Ma Taproot yelled back. 'And what does your brother say about that? Does he care as much for your precious Lora as you do?'

'Of course he does. She's family! Family is very important to us Robinsons.'

'I wonder,' said Ma Taproot more quietly. Now she was at the bottom of the tree and surrounded by her Sentinels, who were staring at the newcomers with bright black eyes.

Ma Taproot was making a meal of how difficult it was for her to walk her heavy bulk around. She was making herself seem more infirm than she actually was. 'I wonder if your Thomas really cares so much about that little girl. And I wonder whether he hasn't seized this opportunity for reasons of his own.'

Uncle Thomas stepped forward. He was in his strange, soldier-type garb, with a massive hat and goggles, and all kinds of weapons strapped to his body.

'Just what is that supposed to mean?' he said. 'You think I would venture into this terrible place if it wasn't to help save the life of my dear, darling niece?'

Even from where I was standing I knew he was insincere. His eyes were blazing with excitement and eagerness. He was astonished by his own bravery in coming all this way underground.

'Run away, you silly little man,' Ma Taproot told him. 'For years you've been too terrified to venture into my realm. You've kept your distance. You've spread wicked lies about me. You've been too yellow-bellied to come anywhere near, and that's suited me fine. But tonight you've got brave, have you? Tonight you come waking an old woman up…'

'We want to know that Lora is safe!' Grandma shrieked, still using the megaphone, even though Ma Taproot was standing just ten yards in front of her.

'I'm safe!' I yelled, hurrying down from the tree. 'I'm fine, look!' Toaster made a grab for me, and tried to hold me back. The Sentinels came shushing along with me, like a strange and silent set of bodyguards. 'Grandma, I'm alive. Ma Taproot is helping us. She fed us, and gave us a place to stay…'

Grandma stared at me, as if she thought I might be some kind of illusion. 'You can't trust her, Lora. Thomas says so.'

'What does he know?' I burst out. '*He* locked me up! He doesn't care what happens to me!'

Thomas was pulling furious, twisted faces at me. I could see at once that he hated my guts, even more than he hated Ma Taproot. That old man might have been related to me, but at that moment he couldn't have cared less if Ma Taproot had cooked me in a stew and eaten me that very evening. No, she was right. He had come here for his own, selfish reasons.

'The tree,' he said, gazing past us. His voice had gone hoarse. His eyes were transfixed by the sight of Ma Taproot's home. 'The tree is actually real.'

'Oh yes,' said Ma Taproot. 'Did you doubt it, Thomas?'

'You will take me to it,' he said. 'I must see inside.' When nobody leapt into action at his words, he shouted: 'At once! I demand that you do what I say! No more diversions! No more fireworks and nonsense. Show me your secrets. Show me the Tree of All Knowledge.'

Ma Taproot laughed softly. 'Never.'

Then he was brandishing a gun in either hand. 'I said, show me the tree. Or you're all dead.'

I didn't believe Ma Taproot was the sort to be intimidated by a show of firearms. I thought she'd sprinkle some kind of magic on him and make those weapons fly away in a bang and a flash of sparkles. But to my surprise she appeared to give in.

'Very well,' she smiled, that old face creasing right up.

We made quite a procession, returning to the tree. All the Servos were commanded to wait at the bottom. It would have taken hours for that lot to go clanking and heaving their clunky selves up the wooden steps.

There was a dicey moment when Uncle Thomas clapped eyes on Watt.

'You betrayer! What are you doing with this lot?'

'I am Watt! Watt I am!' squealed Watt, clicking his switch wildly.

'How dare you abscond with our prisoners!' growled the ruler of Bandit Town.

Watt was almost fainting with fear, but Uncle Thomas just laughed at him, and strode on by. In seconds he'd already forgotten about Watt again, but the lampstand was quivering and flickering for ages afterwards.

I tried to reassure him. 'He's just a nasty bully. You're safe with us, Watt.'

'I should never have left my home,' Watt said. 'What was I thinking of, coming on adventures? I should have stayed just where I was…'

'We could all say that,' I said, picking him up and carrying him in my arms the rest of the way up the winding steps. 'But I guess we didn't. We have to be clever and brave and smart, Watt. That's what my grandma once told me.'

Though at that moment I didn't think my grandma was being any of those things. She was acting very pleased with herself, putting on her high-and-mighty voice as we arrived in Ma Taproot's cosy sitting room.

'Well, look at all this,' Grandma gasped. 'You seem to live an elegant life, even under the ground. Even underneath that stinkin' swamp. Ha!' Then she started poking around the shelves of old books, shoving her nose in rudely.

Uncle Thomas still had his weapons trained on Ma Taproot. 'I guess it's about time you told me the secret of this place. This is the Tree of All Knowledge, isn't it?'

The huge old woman sighed, and sat down carefully on her favourite chair. 'If you like. That's what it's been called by those few who have come this way, over the years. That's one of the legends that's grown up about it.'

Uncle Thomas had a greedy gleam in his eye.

'I don't get this,' I interrupted. Everyone was talking about this tree like it was famous or something. Or some kind of myth. 'I've never heard of this before.'

Peter said, 'Even in the City Inside there's talk about the Tree of All Knowledge. But it's just a rumour. It's crazy. It's supposed to be a tree that was brought from another world and that, miraculously, has been able to grow here…'

'Is it from Earth?' I asked.

Toaster shook his head solemnly. 'No, this isn't any kind of tree native to Earth. Nor Mars. This is from another planet altogether. One I don't know anything about.' There was a deep note in his voice. It was like slow excitement.

My own head was whirling softly now. I'd never even thought about life happening on another planet *besides* Earth or Mars… I had a dizzy feeling: like the universe was opening up all around me…

'There is no secret to this tree,' Ma Taproot said. 'There's nothing you can demand, or bully out of me or steal from us.' She sneered at him. 'So, tough cheese.'

Uncle Thomas snapped: 'Well, then. What's in all those books, huh? They look like they might have secrets in them…'

It was strange to be in the presence of so many old-fashioned, papery books. I hadn't seen books arrayed like that since I was in the City Inside and saw Dean Swiftnick's study and the fancy home of the Graveley family. They were like tiny coffins lined up on the curved walls.

It was hard not to imagine them whispering softly behind our backs, scandalised by the night's events.

Grandma was already over there, yanking them down from their shelves, leafing through volume after volume. She chucked them down in disgust, one after another, every now and then showing us pages of strange, jagged lettering and symbols.

'These are no use to us. It's just gibberish. We can't read this.'

'Whose language is that?' asked Peter. 'It's like the writing on the tunnel walls…' He looked keenly at Ma Taproot. 'Does it belong to another race? Someone we don't even know about yet?'

The old woman chuckled and the old turkey wattles of her neck were wobbling with amusement. 'You're clever, Peter. You're more clever than anyone gives you credit for, boy. Yeah, these histories are written in a language that's dead to most folk still living. Except me, of course. And my friends.'

'Your friends?' Uncle Thomas sneered. 'What friends?'

She waved a gnarled hand to indicate the greyish, snub-nosed beings who followed her everywhere. The Sentinels. They issued forth at her gesture and stood around her like a harmless platoon.

'These? These are just some kinda vermin,' said Thomas. He reached out with the toe of his boot to kick one of the small beings.

'They're just your servants, ain't they?' Grandma cried. She looked at the strange creatures with disgust. 'Horrible-looking things, if you ask me. Like little burden beasts, but less useful.'

I was amazed by my elders' reactions to the Sentinels. Even though they didn't say anything, or do much, I found them a reassuring presence. From my very first sight of them I had found them oddly calming.

'They are my friends,' said Ma Taproot again. 'And you would do well to respect them.'

'They can read these books of lore on your shelves?' asked Thomas eagerly. 'And you can, too?'

'Of course,' Ma Taproot said. 'And yes, in your vulgar parlance, I guess you'd say this library of mine contained secrets. Perhaps all the secrets that Mars will ever have.'

'Oh hoh!' cried my uncle Thomas. 'I had a feeling! I knew this would happen! Didn't I say, Margaret? Didn't I promise?'

I hated the way my older relations were behaving. Greedy and disrespectful.

'What's the matter with you?' I asked. 'What would you do with any kind of secrets, anyhow?'

He whirled round on me: 'Oh, will you just shut it? I've had about enough of you, brat. You may be my sister's granddaughter but I ain't got no time for you whatsoever.'

Grandma wasn't having this. 'Thomas! Now, you leave her alone…!'

He huffed and growled and brandished his guns some more. He didn't scare me one bit.

He returned to demanding stuff from Ma Taproot, who clearly hated him as much as I was starting to. 'You'll tell us what's written here, lady. You'll tell me everything I want to know.'

She laughed in his face. Guns couldn't scare her. 'I don't think my friends would be very happy about that.'

'Nuts to your friends!' growled Uncle Thomas.

'Uh, Thomas…' said my grandma warningly. Her voice had gone high and wavering.

'What is it?' he snapped.

By now we could all see what was happening.

Every single one of those knee-high creatures had stepped forward. They were surrounding him and gazing up at him as one with those dark, unblinking eyes.

Together they were emitting a blue shining light.

'Oh dear,' said Ma Taproot. 'I'm afraid you've annoyed them.'

There was a crackle of that sapphire light and a crash, and the next thing we knew, Uncle Thomas had collapsed on the floor in a crumpled heap.

9

'Oh my god! What have you done? Have you killed him?'

Grandma was suddenly on her hands and knees. She pummelled at Thomas' chest with her fists and put her ear to his face to check he was still breathing.

Ma Taproot snorted with amusement. 'He'll live. Probably. But it's as well that he's quiet for a while. He was getting on my nerves.'

The Sentinels were still gathered in a circle around us. A weird kind of power was emanating from them. They no longer seemed small and harmless.

Peter gave me a strange look, as if he was asking me what the hell had we got ourselves into. And the truth was: I didn't know.

'If you've hurt my brother I swear, I'll…' Grandma squared up to our hostess.

'You'll what?' laughed Ma Taproot. 'You do like shouting your mouth off, don't you, Margaret Robinson? I think you've started to believe the things that others say about you. All about how important you are. The last living Earth Woman. Pah.' Ma Taproot sneered at her. 'Well, I don't think you're such great shakes. Your granddaughter here is worth ten of you.'

'I don't doubt that,' said Grandma shakily. 'She was never much when she was growing up. Just a scrawny-looking tomboy. I always thought more of her brother. But I guess she's proved herself enough in recent times.'

'She certainly has,' nodded the old woman who lived in the tree. 'And I believe she's fit to undergo the next stage in her mission.'

'But my brother … is he okay? Is he alive?'

'Of course,' Ma Taproot spared him a quick glance. 'The Ancients aren't given to killing other sentient beings. Not so offhandedly and callously anyway. That's the way human beings carry on.'

Peter jerked like a puppet. 'The who? The what did you say?'

Ma Taproot gave one of her massive smiles, and her whole face uncrumpled, showing off a weird inner light.

'Ah, you understand me, do you, Peter? Yes, you're the clever one. You're always quickest on the uptake. Sometimes it makes you impulsive and you get things wrong. But you are clever and Lora is brave and Toaster is loyal. Those are your best qualities.'

Peter wasn't going to be distracted by her compliments and neither was I. We had both heard what she had called the small beings that were clustered around us.

'The Ancients,' Peter was saying now, staring at them.

'You called them … the Ancients. What does that actually mean?'

Ma Taproot chuckled, and it was as if a mellow, warm breeze was issuing through that library room. A shushing noise rippled through the crowd of calm Sentinel creatures. Were they all laughing gently at our puzzlement? It wasn't malicious laughter. It wasn't like that. But they were looking at us, kind of waiting for us to catch up with the joke.

'They're wicked things,' Grandma spat. 'They've done something horrible to my brother. They've robbed him of his senses. And he's an old man, too. His old heart probably can't take such a strain…'

'Hush,' said Ma Taproot gently. 'Hush now, Margaret. Your brother is fine. And you must be quiet now.'

'Must I?' bellowed Grandma. 'Why, there's an army of Servos outside, waiting below, at the bottom of this tree. They belong to my brother and I'm sure they'd do anything I command.' Her expression turned sly and nasty. 'Why, I could make them attack. They could rip this dump apart. These hideous little creatures of yours just wouldn't stand a chance…!'

'I hope you wouldn't do anything of the sort,' said Ma Taproot, in a warning kind of voice.

'Grandma, please,' I said, knowing the signs for Grandma when she was about to fly into one of her rages.

Grandma was looking pleased with the attention she

was getting now. 'I could yell out of the window. And they'd all come running. All those robots with their grabby hands and weapons and their lasers and cutting tools. They'd trash this place, and you'd all deserve it too! And Toaster! You'd do what I say, too, wouldn't you? You've always done everything I've told you…'

There was a flicker that filled all of Toaster's screens. He looked like he wished she wasn't asking him this stuff. His voice came out strained-sounding: 'Margaret, you're wrong. I wouldn't attack these people, no matter what you said. Ma Taproot is not our enemy. Nor are … these beings that she called the *Ancients*.'

She looked so upset then, my grandma. All of a sudden she looked old and tiny and stranded by herself at the other side of the room, hunkered over her brother's still body.

I felt bad for her because she was still my grandma, but I knew she was wrong. Causing a ruckus here would be the wrong thing to do. We were here now and we had to learn what Ma Taproot had in mind for us. For good or bad.

'Lora, you don't know anything about these creatures,' said Grandma.

'But we have to trust them, Grandma. If we want to carry on with our mission. If I want to find Ma and Hannah. Ma Taproot will know which way to go.'

And Ma Taproot did. At my words, she gently took

command of the situation again, ushering us away from my angry grandma and calling the small creatures around us. 'They will show you the way.'

I was looking much more warily at the small, pale-skinned beings now. Grandma had been right when she said they resembled the burden beasts we had been used to on the prairie. But their skins were much paler, less leathery, and they stood on two legs. Also, now I looked, a brilliant intelligence could be seen in those dark, twinkling eyes.

I asked Ma Taproot: 'When you called them the Ancients, did you really mean it? Are these really the people who we've been looking for? Are they the oldest living people on Mars?'

'Oh yes, indeed,' Ma Taproot told us. 'They're a lot more talkative when they're in their own realm, however. Up here in my tree they're content to play quietly and be my Sentinels. Aren't they wonderful?'

'*Up* here?' asked Peter. 'But we're deep underground. How can this be up?'

She smiled. 'Because they dwell in a kingdom much deeper under the surface of Mars. And that is where you must allow them to take you.'

I was looking at the gentle faces of the Ancients gathered around us. They were smooth and their expressions hardly altered. But I thought I could trust them. I was ready to follow them, and so was Peter. And

I was sure that Toaster, Watt and Karl would be loyal enough to come with us, wherever we were taken next.

Down into the heart of Mars.

Ma Taproot nodded happily. Behind her Grandma let out a squawk of protest.

'No! Not my granddaughter! You can't have her! Where are you taking her? Lora! Don't go with them…!'

Now Ma Taproot was lumbering towards the far wall of that curved room. There was a door in the vast trunk of the tree that I'd not noticed before. It was cunningly disguised within the bookcases. She pressed a switch and the door swung open.

'It's time to be moving on,' she told us. 'The Ancients are happy to take you down, into their world. You must go right now, though. With no further delay.'

'But… what about Grandma?'

Ma Taproot gave me a rueful smile. 'She will be safe here, with us. I promise you that, Lora.'

I nodded. 'We'll be back soon,' I told Grandma, who suddenly looked more ancient than any of the Sentinel creatures clustered around us. She made a futile gesture with her hands as if she could draw me back to her.

But she couldn't. I was on my way. Deeper into the heart of Mars.

'You must go now,' said Ma Taproot.

'We will,' I said.

Beyond was a small, smooth-walled antechamber.

We had to squash up to get inside. Peter had both Karl and a worried-looking Watt in his arms. He frowned at me, wondering what we were getting ourselves into. I wasn't sure at all, but I knew we were doing the right thing. We had to carry on our quest.

Doors closed silently, sealing us off from Ma Taproot's room.

Toaster was taking up quite a lot of the space with his angular bulk. The old sunbed was radiating a terrible sorrow at leaving Grandma behind. He had chosen us over her, in the end.

'She'll be all right, Toaster, and so will Uncle Thomas.'

'I am responsible for the whole Robinson family,' Toaster said, in an agonised voice. 'I have been responsible for so many years. Thomas ... essentially ... created me. He gave me blue-chip technology to augment my mind. He gave me this body. I'd be long gone without him by now.'

The small creatures were standing with us and they were completely silent. There were seven of them in that small room. The Ancients, Ma Taproot had called them. We had thought they were simply servants. Lowly beings, who couldn't even speak. How wrong we were, and how embarrassed I now felt, having dismissed them like this.

Suddenly I felt tongue-tied in their presence. They gazed up at me with those soft eyes and those gentle smiles and I felt all the anxiety draining out of me.

'Are you really…?' I started to say, and one of them put a finger to its rounded snout, as if to say: not yet. There'll be time for answers later.

All at once the room we were in started to move. It gave a lurch and Karl yelped with alarm.

I knew what was happening!

We were in an elevator!

It was moving just like the ones in Stockpot House, which we discovered when we first arrived in the City Inside. My brother and I had loved those magical devices. We could hardly believe they existed: whizzing so rapidly up and down the two hundred storeys of our gleaming glass home.

An elevator! One that began in the trunk of Ma Taproot's tree and went down and down much deeper than the roots.

Unimaginably far down into the crust and boiling magma of Mars. Because this journey was taking a long time.

And we were speeding up, too.

We gripped the walls and each other for support. The metal walls were vibrating. Toaster suction-clamped his sturdy feet to the floor and we grabbed hold of him when he told us to.

Watt almost lost control: blinking his light bulb and shouting out his name at the top of his voice.

Meanwhile the Ancients were showing no signs of alarm whatsoever. They were singing, I realised. It was a high-pitched, humming song. Gradually they were changing colour, too, from pale grey to a bluish purple and then into a pale orange. The quality of the air around them was rippling. There was a golden glow about them, as if they were changing their very essence, somehow, before our eyes.

'Lora, what have we got ourselves into?' Peter shouted, over the increasing whine of the elevator. His eyes were bulging out in shock and he'd gone a very pale shade of green. 'We're gonna die!'

'I don't think so,' I tried to tell him and, all at once, I wanted to laugh. Just look at us! Look where we were going! We were hurtling into the very heart of Mars!

Look what was happening to us!

Had any human beings ever come this far?

'I am Watt! Watt I am!'

'Hold tight, everyone,' said Toaster calmly. 'Something is happening … something … very … very… strange…'

The Ancients were glowing blue and gold and they were growing, or we were shrinking, or both. They had become tall, angelic beings. I could see their features better now, as they loomed over us. They carried on smiling, encouragingly.

When they smiled they revealed razor-sharp teeth.

'Toaster, make it stop!' Peter yelled.

'How can I?' he shouted back. 'There's nothing we can do. We're in their hands…'

The noise of the elevator changed pitch, and we were slowing. We arrived at the bottom of the shaft with a cushioned thump.

We looked up at the Ancients. The seven of them were graceful, long-limbed, beautiful creatures. You couldn't tell if they were women or men or what kind of clothes they were wearing. They were about twenty feet tall now, it seemed, and their expressions were so far away they were hard to read.

'At least we can't see those teeth anymore,' Peter muttered.

They had, for just a second, looked completely terrifying. But right now they were back to being peaceful and serene. I realised that we'd better remember that whatever the Ancients looked like, they had those deadly hidden fangs.

I jumped when one of them spoke.

'This is where we live. You've arrived.'

And the doors slid open again.

I could barely restrain myself. 'This is it? We've made it? This is the place we were looking for?'

We were led into a golden corridor. What were the walls and floor made out of? It looked like flame, but it was hard to the touch, even though it rippled as we were led along.

'Welcome,' said the Ancient who had spoken.

I stared up at him, but his face was so far away it was

102

hard to catch his eye and demand answers. But I had to try. 'My mother,' I said. 'And my sister. Are they here?'

'Welcome,' said the Ancient again, and the others joined in saying the same word over and over until it became a chant.

Or maybe I should call it a lullaby. Because the next thing I knew I had fallen asleep.

And time passed.

10

The door swished open and my mother was standing there, on the other side, in a small room.

It took me a moment to realise that it was truly her.

She didn't quite look like herself. She had some sort of garish colours painted on her face and her long, dark hair had been cut into a shorter style. She smiled at me, shyly.

Her clothes were so nondescript. They were like a plain uniform in some kind of plastic material, I had been given the same. She was never one for fussy dressing, but when I pictured her she was always in something pretty and feminine with puffy sleeves. Something worn and old, but clean.

She didn't hug me. When I moved forward, into her room, lifting up my arms, she backed away. She warded me off, like I was a bad spirit.

'M-ma?'

It was too much to take in all at once. The sight of her again. The fact that our mission had succeeded! The way she looked so different. And now the worried look on her face. Refusing to let me come anywhere near. I got a hollow clutch of pain in my stomach as we both stood there, frozen and awkward.

'Lora, please, sit down. Let me explain.'

There was only one chair in the small room. But, even as I thought this, a second chair simply grew out of the floor, curved and smooth like the other one. It rose up beside me magically and waited invitingly for me to sit. I did so, uneasily.

These people – the Ancients – are powerful, I thought. They have technology we can barely comprehend. They can do things that are astounding.

'Ma?' I said. 'It's me. Lora.'

'I know.' She smiled gently. 'Don't you think I'd know my own daughter?'

'But…' I still had a hollow feeling inside. My mouth was sour. Where were the tears and the smiles and the laughter? And the rushing to spill out our stories? Where was the huge feeling of relief? Where was the feeling of coming home? Everything I had imagined it would be like, seeing Ma again. The way I had hoped it might be. It wasn't quite coming true.

'Where's Hannah?' I asked.

'She's safe, Lora. You will see her soon. You must calm down. There is nothing bad or wicked here. You can relax. You are on your guard, I can tell.'

On my guard? Well, of course I was.

Ma looked at me quizzically. Her face was all orange and blue with powder and paint.

'What's going on, Ma?'

'This is my home, Lora. I'm used to it here now. I don't even know how long has gone by. I guess … months? As much as a year? Or more? You look older…'

'I do?'

She nodded. And when I thought about it, I wasn't sure how much time had passed, either. How long exactly was it since we loaded just a few of our belongings on the hovercart and left our Homestead behind?

'This place…' I began.

'Isn't it just like a miracle?' she smiled. Her whole face glowed at the thought.

Ma's room was oddly shaped. It was a sphere with flattened sides. It interlocked with many other cells.

When I looked at the softly glowing walls I realised that I could see other dim shapes moving behind the translucent walls.

Other bodies! More people! They moved about only slightly in their confines. It was like we were sitting in a honeycomb.

I remembered the nests of metallic insects in the woods where we once lived, when I was so small. Da showed me how to extract the green honey and I remembered the taste. The air here was filled with a similar sweetness. Too much sweetness.

The door into Ma's tiny parlour was merely one among many.

Ma was speaking again and I was only half-listening.

She was breathlessly demonstrating the buttons and switches and electronic panels in the walls around her. Her hands moved surely across them, adjusting the lighting and the atmospheric noise in her room.

At her touch faces and pictures appeared, glowing on the walls.

She turned to me, to check out how impressed I was. And I was! It was almost like magic. She was so confident in the way she could work it all. I must have looked so surprised.

Music came from nowhere: strange and discordant. She laughed at my confused expression. I watched her fingers dance expertly on control panels that only phased into existence when she went to touch them.

'We had nothing like this in the City Inside,' I said. 'I mean, the things we saw there were incredible. Super advanced and amazing. I'd never seen the like. But this is different again…'

'Ah, yes,' Ma turned to me, smiling. 'Yes, I heard about your City Inside. That's where you went, isn't it? That's where they took you. The Martian Ghost girl flew you there. And you left us behind.'

'They separated us, Ma,' I protested. 'I wanted to keep us all together. The whole lot of us. I'd never have left you and Hannah behind willingly. And look! I've come all this way, looking for you.'

'I know,' she nodded calmly. 'I know more about what's been going on than you would imagine.'

'You do?'

'Oh yes. This … apparatus of the Ancient Ones. Their wonderful machinery. It can tune into your thoughts and your desires. It can show you pictures from halfway across Mars. I've had fleeting glimpses of what's been going on. A few pictures. I've had an idea of what's been happening…'

I stared at her face, trying to gauge her emotions. If Ma had been disturbed or worried about our adventures in the past few months, she showed little sign of it. She was placid and smiling slightly. She looked very pleased with herself.

'Are you a prisoner here, Ma?'

'I wouldn't call it that, no,' she said. 'Though whether I am free to leave or not, I do not know. I haven't asked.'

'What?'

'I'm quite content here, Lora.' She held up her hands. 'Look how soft my skin is now. No, stay there. Don't touch. Don't come near. You remember my hands, don't you? Scarred and hard from years of working. And my face. I was old before my time. Living in those scouring desert winds. Picking corn till my hands were lashed and cut and dyed with the blue juice. I spent every single day cleaning dishes and knives in red sand and all my skin was dry and hard. Look, now. Soft. So soft. There's no wind here. No dust storms. Nothing to disturb my peace.'

I realised my mouth was hanging open. 'But it's a prison cell, Ma. They've got you locked up!'

'And I'm happy to stay here forever. All my needs are met. I am quite content. They bring me my blue pills, which I still need. They will see to it that I never run out. And they feed me delicious food, which I don't have to prepare. And occasionally I see pictures of what is happening to those I love, elsewhere in the world. Isn't that enough for me? Why shouldn't that be enough?'

I didn't know how to answer her. In a way I was glad that she was so content and well looked after. Out on the prairie, and when we were travelling through the wilderness, she hadn't been happy at all.

Perhaps Ma had found her safe place in the world at last. Her family didn't need her now. I didn't need her now. Perhaps she deserved to relax here, in this room where everything takes care of her.

I was struggling to think what to say when the door swished open again and one of the Ancients slipped in quietly. This one was back in the same, squat, smooth form of the Sentinels in Ma Taproot's tree.

'Lora,' it said, and I jumped, because I wasn't used to the Sentinel creatures speaking. 'I am to look after you personally. It has been agreed. My name is…' The creature seemed to be choosing a human name it thought I might like … 'Arnold.'

His voice was soft, fluting, whispering. 'You must leave your mother. She will be fatigued by now.'

Ma nodded. 'It's true. I am. See how they care for me?'

Arnold added, 'If you want to meet your little sister, then we can go right now.'

'All right,' I said, somehow trusting his gentle voice.

'Goodbye, Lora,' Ma said, with a shy little wave.

Hannah was the baby of our family.

In spite of my strange meeting with Ma, I was expecting Hannah to be the same small self I'd last seen so many months before.

Back when she first learned to walk she used to come running to me and Al and grab us round the knees, hugging herself to us, like she'd never let us go. She'd look up at us and seem so fierce with her love. I used to wonder how she could contain so much life and personality in such a small body.

I had been missing her for months. When I focused my thoughts and counted up, it must have been more than a year. Time was strangely dilated in the City Inside, as it was here, I now understood. It seemed all too easy to lose track.

I was so excited to see my sister again.

The Sentinel led me to another room and opened the cell door. I whirled round and looked at him.

'You've made a mistake,' I said. 'You've brought me to the wrong room…'

His small black eyes blinked slowly at me.

The young girl sitting in the middle of the glowing cell

simply laughed, and the Ancient One behind me chuckled along with her.

'There's no mistake, Lora. Come in. Sit here with me.' She smiled at me before speaking to Arnold, the Sentinel. 'She'll realise soon. She's just mixed up, that's all. She's been through a lot. No wonder she doesn't recognise me.'

The small Ancient padded out of the room and the door shut smoothly. I was alone with this girl who was claiming to be my sister, though she was much too grown up. She was in a plain overall just like my mother, and her hair was cut short, just the same.

She looked like me.

As I stared at her, studying her carefully, I realised that I was looking at my own face. My face as it had been before the dust storms came down, and the Disappearances started, before we were driven away from our prairie home. It was a face with no worries or concerns, very like the one that I remembered looking at in the cracked, burnished mirror of our old bathroom. I had left this face far behind, somewhere on all my journeys and adventures, and now my sister was wearing it.

'How old are you?' I asked her. 'Y-you can't be Hannah. She'd only be … six?'

She nodded. 'Yes, that's what I am. Why don't you recognise me, Lora?' There was a line between her eyebrows as she frowned at me. I knew this expression at once: it was the one she wore when things weren't going exactly the way she wanted them to.

'But you were a baby the last time I saw you. Ma was still carrying you in her arms...'

She smiled. 'Yes, during our epic journey across the wilderness, of course she did. She was very protective. She hugged me to her as much as she could. She was comforting herself and me. We didn't know what we were going to face next, did we? Shadow Beasts. Martian Ghosts. Lizard Birds...'

As she said these things, it all seemed like a hundred years ago. We had all got a lot older and wiser since then, I thought.

'But ... your speech,' I told her, still not completely convinced. 'It's perfect. It's so grown up...'

'Yes,' she frowned. 'I'm aware of that, and I'm sorry if you find it disconcerting...'

'Disconcerting!' I laughed. I stared at her sitting there, with her still-podgy little girl hands resting on her lap. 'Listen to the words you're using! Where did you learn words like that?'

'Why, right here,' she replied calmly. 'Mother and I have had the privilege of months spent living with the Ancients in this realm. I have learned a great deal. My mind has advanced so much and so, I believe, has our mother's, though I haven't seen her for some weeks. This is a truly wonderful place, Lora. The Ancients are a marvellous people. They have so much to offer us.'

I gawped at her. 'You haven't seen Ma for weeks?!'

'There's been no need to. We both have much to do. Much to learn. We were so far behind, you see. Our minds were hungry. Mine is still relatively new. This young brain sucks up knowledge so beautifully. The Ancients are very pleased with my progress. And Ma – well, you know our ma. For many years, in our previous life on the prairie, she was little more than a domestic drudge. Just a husk of a person. She neglected her mind and her creative, intellectual self. She was so very frustrated and furious inside.'

'She was?'

'Oh, yes. That's why she took all those pills that she used to get from the Adams' Emporium. Do you remember? She would ask for them, looking shame-faced, and Mrs Adams would scoop them out of a big glass jar…'

Of course I remembered. But I hadn't expected Hannah to know about such grown-up mysteries.

'The pills calmed her down,' Hannah said. 'They soothed her fervid imaginings and her frustrations. And she needs them still, though the Ancients are weaning her off them. They are teaching her. They are feeding her mind and every day she gets better in her spirit and her soul.'

I looked round for somewhere to sit and, as before, a chair mushroomed out of nowhere beside me. 'This is all too much to take in. We came here, you know, on a quest, my friends and me. We came here to rescue you both…'

'I know,' said Hannah. 'And don't think that we don't appreciate it, Lora. I know that you imagined that we were in terrible straits. Ma being helpless and terrified. Me being barely more than a toddler. Both of us at the mercy of terrible beasts in the Underworld…' Hannah laughed gaily at the very thought of this. 'But as you can see, dear sister, we are both more than safe and happy. We are content. We are fulfilled. We are seeking enlightenment.'

I gasped at this. Enlightenment? What was she talking about?

'They've done something to you,' I told her. 'They've messed with your mind. This isn't right. None of this.'

'But it is, Lora. It's perfection.'

'I'm going to take you away from this.'

She shook her head. 'No,' she said.

And then Arnold came to take *me* away again, back to my own cell, where my friends were waiting.

'You'll see, sister,' said Hannah, as I was leaving. 'We have everything here. And tomorrow, when I'm rested, I will show you something to convince you. You will see that you never need to be anywhere but here, at the very heart of our world.'

11

I wasted no time in telling the others what was going on. We gathered in another of those translucent rooms, though the whispering Ancients had promised that soon we would each have one of our own.

'You were ages,' Peter said. 'We were thinking you'd been Disappeared…'

I shuddered. 'I wish I had been. Instead I saw Ma and Hannah and I almost wish I hadn't.'

They stared at me, amazed.

I told them how much Ma and Hannah had changed. How I might not even have recognised them if I'd bumped into them with no warning.

'Everyone changes so much,' said Toaster, in his saddest and deepest voice. 'I've learned that. It's something you find out when you live a life as long as mine.'

'But … there's changing naturally, in a way to suit your life,' I said, feeling angry all of a sudden. 'And there's being *made* to change. There are forced changes. And they can't even see them. They can't even tell that they've been changed against their wills. They don't even know they're *prisoners* here. They're comfortable and warm and fed ... and now they don't want to be anywhere else.'

Peter was looking wistful. 'I can see the advantages, I must admit.' He went back to lounge on one of those weird chairs that simply grew out of the floor when you needed one. Karl leapt onto his lap, circled twice, and flomped down to sleep. 'I mean, we've been through some tough times. We've barely rested. And when we did, it was always somewhere dangerous and inhospitable. I imagine your mother and sister felt just the same way. You should cut them some slack. Let them enjoy their rest.'

I gawped at him. 'But doesn't this place ring any alarm bells for you? Don't you think it seems wrong?'

He blinked at me. 'Hmm?' I could see he was drifting off to sleep.

Toaster said, 'You are distrustful, Lora, and it is no wonder. After our experiences in the City Inside, where we were welcomed and given luxurious quarters, and encouraged to settle ourselves in our new environment. Why, even I was hoodwinked into believing we were safe. I can appreciate why you would be suspicious of the Ancient Ones and their world here.'

I should have known Toaster would understand. We had been through so much together. I pushed aside my annoyance at Peter (who was now completely asleep, with Karl dozing on top of him).

'It was just so disappointing, Toaster. I thought they'd

116

both be much more glad to see me. But Ma and Hannah … they hardly seemed bothered at all. They seemed like they didn't care either way about our family any more…'

Toaster commiserated. But what else could he say? The ways of humans were often a mystery to him. We behaved very oddly, he always thought. It was his job to go round picking up the pieces after each of our disasters. He had to keep putting us back together again.

'Hey, where's Watt?' I asked, noticing that the small lamp was missing.

'I am Watt! Watt I am!' He came bustling into the room as though he'd heard me asking for him. He was cheery and excitable. I hadn't heard the electronic door whooshing open.

'Where did you come from?'

'Just exploring,' he said, airily. His light bulb fizzed and glared. 'Just having a nose around.' He seemed evasive. But I was too tired to pursue the point. A very comfortable-looking couch rose out of the floor beside me, and I lay down gratefully and slept for a full ten hours.

The lights dimmed around me as I fell asleep, and Toaster set himself to recharge. It was nice and quiet in that softly luminous cell, just as it was in all the ones around us, in every direction. There was a steady hum that might have been some kind of energy, or it might have been singing, somewhere far away.

When I woke up Peter and Karl were gone. So was Watt.

Toaster calmed me down when I started to panic. 'Don't, Lora. It's fine. You slept through. But the Ancients came and took them away to a room of their own, where they will be very comfortable. It isn't anything sinister.'

'No?' I snapped. 'Then where are they? How do we find them again?'

Toaster didn't know. His face wore a sorrowful expression, flickering with self-doubt. 'You are correct. I was distracted. I should have paid more attention. I let them take our friends away. I was hooked up to their power source and enjoying it too much. And I was accessing their databanks and … and … it's glorious, Lora. I can't get full access to their stores. But they have let me into the shallows. I have stared into the wilder seas and the distant horizons. They have so much here. There is so much to know.'

'Are they going to let you swim out?' I asked him. I could sense the excitement in the old sunbed. Nothing got him worked up as much as new knowledge, in any forms. Back in our Homestead and Our Town he had learned everything there was to know. He had been growing rusted and jaded. Then our adventures and explorations had brought him back to life. Everything we had encountered had boosted and stimulated him. His thirst for new knowledge was boundless.

'Swim?' he asked. 'I … I … don't know. They are letting

me stand in shallow waters and they are tempting me. Yes. That's the word. Tempting.'

He fell quiet and then one of the Ancients came knocking for me on the sliding door. It was Arnold again. 'Come with me,' he said.

Did he smile then? It was hard to tell.

That morning I made my second visit to Hannah. She had promised to show me something special.

When I entered her room she was sitting calmly and expectantly. She was wearing exactly the same outfit as the day before.

'You're still in old rags,' she observed. 'You should let the Ancients give you something new to wear.'

'I wouldn't wear what they've given you,' I said. 'I don't like the colour.'

Hannah told me to sit down and she waved her arms at the walls around us. Her fingers flickered and gestured as if in sign language, giving subtle commands to unseen sensors. The glowing walls rippled like liquid and certain patches in the air glowed more fiercely than ever. And then there were pictures forming in the air.

'Now,' said Hannah. 'Didn't I tell you that we don't need to go anywhere? We can see the whole of Mars while we're sitting right here. Watch this, Lora. And then you'll know just how much we know, and how much the Ancient Ones know about all of us…'

The first thing I saw made the words die in my throat. The pictures were so vivid and three-dimensional. I'd seen nothing like them. Not even the devices in the City Inside created pictures inside your room as real as this.

They were impossible, surely…

Here was Grandma. She was with Thomas, in his globular helmet and tattered space suit, and his crew of battered Servo-Furnishings. They had retreated to the swamplands above ground. I could almost smell the fetid, creeping mist that hung around the trees. Grandma looked haggard with worry and her brother had his arm over her shoulders. Were those tears in her eyes?

'She's weeping about you, Lora,' Hannah told me. 'She thinks she's lost you forever. When the Ancients came and took you away, she thought you were going to your doom.' Hannah laughed, like the whole thing was a game. As if Grandma was just being silly.

She waved her hand at the screen and the image melted away. It was soon replaced by an image of Ruby in her ramshackle town of wooden houses. They were on their knees and they were praying. I guessed from the way they were howling and carrying on that they were beseeching some far-off deity for mercy.

'Her father would be so disappointed in her,' Hannah said. 'I heard he was a Star engineer, and that he hoped she would grow up logical and scientific. But her head is filled with crazy stuff and superstitious nonsense. She worships the Ancient Ones and she hardly knows anything about them.' Hannah giggled at the awestruck look on Ruby's face as she prayed.

When the picture shifted again, the mists took longer to clear next time. It was as if the machine was reaching across far greater distances to bring back these images.

'It's amazing, Hannah,' I said. 'But how do you know how to work this thing? How can you make it do what you want?'

She looked smug all of a sudden. 'The machines are tuned to my brain waves. It takes months to achieve, and it's dangerous, sometimes. The contact with the Ancients can burn out your entire skull, if you're unlucky. This has happened to others, in the past, and it's very unfortunate. But I am one of the lucky ones.'

'Hang on,' I interrupted. 'What? Who? Have you seen others here?' I felt sick all of a sudden. 'Burned-out skulls…?!'

'Hush,' said Hannah. 'That doesn't matter now…'

'Doesn't matter?'

'You just have to be careful when you're working the machinery,' she said, in a distant voice. 'It's a wonderful thing. It can be dangerous, sure. But it's a wonderful thing.'

My mouth had gone parched. 'I'm sure…'

She grinned. 'And just look what it has done for me! Just look at what I can do!'

Suddenly we were both looking at our brother, Al. He

was twice life-size, on the wall of Hannah's cell. How smart he looked in his formal suit, so typical of the people of the City Inside.

He was walking through crowds of similarly dressed men in the very heart of the City. His shoes were shiny and black, even in the slushy red snow on the pavement.

Carriages and lizards were teeming in the road and snow was falling heavily and it came as some surprise to see how very busy it was in the City. In the past few weeks I had almost forgotten the crush of those streets. In a way I almost missed it.

Al couldn't see us watching him, of course. He was simply going about his business with the rest of the crowd, looking exactly like he fitted in.

'What do you think he would say, Lora? If he could see me here and now?' Hannah asked. 'His baby sister, sounding and looking so different? So grown up and augmented by the Ancients. I think he'd be proud, don't you? I think he'd be astonished and rather proud of me.'

I turned to look at Hannah. She was so pleased with herself, and just then, even though I'd only just found her again, she made me feel like lashing out.

'Are you sure? You were a nice kid, Hannah. A little girl with a sweet nature. The baby of our family. And they've taken you and made you into a kind of monster … that's what I think, if you really want to know. And that's what Al would think, too.'

'Do you really think so? I'm not sure that you and Al always agreed on important matters. I've seen you disagree on crucial points. In fact, when he met his beloved Tillian in the City Inside, and started living with the Graveley family, you weren't very happy at all, were you? You started yelling and shouting about how he had changed, too.'

I was shocked she knew this. 'Wait a minute… How can you know this stuff? Have you … have you been watching us all along?'

'I think Al would love the way I've changed,' Hannah went on. 'I think he'd say I was a miraculous person. I was better than just some boring normal little girl. I think he'd even say that I was his favourite sister.'

I shrugged, and turned to go. I'd had enough of her stupid games. She might have increased intelligence and mental powers and all, but she was still behaving like a toddler.

I felt like my guts were being wrenched out. I decided I was going to find Ma and ask her what she thought about all of this. It was like we'd lost little Hannah and she had been replaced by this smart-mouthed creature.

'Wait,' Hannah burst out, seeing that I was heading for the door. 'One more picture. I'll let you see one more thing.'

I sighed deeply. 'I don't want to see anything else, thanks, Hannah. Open the door.'

'I think you'll want to see this. Really, I do. It's someone else you want to know about. Someone else you want to know is okay…'

My heart started hammering in my chest. 'What? Who?'

Al melted away and the mists started flowing about on the walls again. The colours were mesmerising, but I didn't let them distract me.

'You know who I mean, Lora,' said Hannah, in her sweet, taunting voice. 'And I wonder what he would think? I wonder if I would be his favourite, too? I think I probably would.'

The image was vague and fuzzy at first. There was clear daylight pouring into a small and messy room. A bedroom. At the window there were metal gantries.

It took me a moment to recognise the walkways that lay outside the windows of the small apartment in the City where I had found Da and Grandma living. That's what we were looking at.

The room was Da's, and the figure on the bed in twisted sheets was Da himself.

He was so pale. Cold sweat was standing out on the pinched flesh of his face. His eyes were looking at phantoms only he could see and he was muttering in his delirium.

'Oh! Hannah! What's wrong with him?' I grabbed hold of her little body, as if I could shake the truth out of her. 'Is this happening now? Is this what's happening to him right now?'

She looked as shocked as I was. 'N-no, it's not immediate. The pictures can't be immediate. They take time to travel … this is recent, though. It isn't too long ago…'

'But he's terribly ill,' I said, staring at the gaunt figure on the screen. 'What's the matter with him? Is he dying?' And then a dreadful thought came to me. 'He could be dead already…'

12

'We have to go to him,' I gasped. 'Don't you see? Da needs our help. We must do whatever we can…'

Suddenly Hannah looked like a little girl again. As young as she truly was. All her clever words abandoned her and she started to cry.

'Oh, Hannah, I'm sorry. I don't mean to scare you. I'm sure Da is all right. I mean I'm sure he can be made well again…' By now the picture had faded from the wall screen, as if it had never been.

Hannah was shaking and sobbing by now. I went to comfort her. 'Oh, honey. Come on, don't worry…'

She held up both hands to ward me off. 'Don't come near me. Stay there, Lora. I don't want your hugs or your fussing over me.'

I felt like I'd been slapped.

'I'm going to have a lie down. You'd better leave me.'

'All right,' I said. 'But we should start making preparations … to leave. It's a long way back to the City Inside.'

Her pale little face stared back at me. She looked incredulous. 'I'm not going anywhere,' she told me. 'And neither are you.'

Of course I went straight to Ma to tell her what we'd learned. My head was reeling. We had all left him behind. All those years he had been there looking after us and now, when he needed his family the most, we were all so far away. I was determined to do everything I could for him.

Ma looked mildly surprised when I said I had seen him. 'You can't have done.'

'Hannah was showing off how she can work the magic pictures. She showed me where he was.'

Ma smiled. 'Hannah has become a very clever girl.'

'Clever?' I shook my head. 'Yeah, I guess. But she's changed, Ma. Surely you can see that? She's become too grown up, too clever for her own good...'

'We are in the machinery,' said Ma, in a distracted sort of voice. 'We all change.'

Her tone of voice niggled at me. She was aggravating me. She looked like she didn't even care about the news I'd passed on about Da.

'He looked like he was dying, Ma.'

She sat placidly in her comfortable chair, which seemed to drift around the room according to her will, as she moved from panel to panel, adjusting levers and switches.

She offered me some mint tea and some sugary biscuits. The news about Da had hardly ruffled her mood at all.

'Ma? Are you even listening to me?'

'Oh, Lora, you mustn't fly into these panics,' Ma sighed. 'You must be sure not to overreact.'

'Overreact!' I stared at her. 'But Da was alone and sick…!'

'Are you sure it was really him? And are you sure about what you saw?'

Why would she try to sow doubt in my mind? Why wasn't she reacting in a normal, natural way? This was more than just the blue pills that calmed her down, I was sure.

'Ma, what's the matter with you? I know what I saw. It was Da. It was your husband. And he was mortally sick. Something terrible has happened while we've been away looking for you…'

Clouds seemed to pass over my mother's perfectly serene face. She studied me and took a deep breath. 'You have to understand about grown-ups, Lora. You're still a little girl. The thing is, your da… I said goodbye to him a long time ago. Remember? He Disappeared on the prairie. It was sad and it was difficult. But he was gone, and we adjusted, didn't we? We struck out on our own and we survived.'

'Yes!' I burst out. 'But he was actually alive! All that time! And I found him again…'

'And I believe you, my love,' Ma sighed. 'I truly do. I believe that you really believe, with all your heart, the things you say you experienced in this City Inside of yours. I am sure that, to you, it was all as real as I am here, sitting before you.'

'What?'

'I do believe you, Lora. You are my eldest daughter. My brave girl. I have every faith in the things you say.'

But every word she was saying now really meant the opposite. She doubted everything I had said about my life since we were parted in the palace of the Lizard Queen. But why? Why would she doubt what I said?

'Ma, I don't understand you...'

'I believe you believe your father still lives, Lora. And Grandma and all the rest of it. I truly believe you when you say you've had these amazing adventures on the surface of the world. I'm your ma, and so I'm bound to believe you, aren't I? But you don't really have any proof, do you?'

'But ... but the pictures on Hannah's wall! This amazing machinery you have down here ... the powers of the Ancients... Come and see... Come to Hannah's room and she'll show you, too.'

'But that won't do any good!' Ma laughed. She actually laughed at me. 'Don't you see? The magic pictures don't necessarily show you the truth, as it is in the world. Didn't Hannah explain to you?'

'No, she didn't...'

'They show things that are in your head. Things that aren't necessarily the literal truth. That's what I believe, anyhow.'

'But you don't know for sure?' I persisted. Could she even be right? Were the pictures just a fantasy? Maybe Da was all right, back there in the City Inside.

I didn't know anything for sure any more.

All at once I wanted to believe what Ma was telling me. I

looked at her gentle face and I wanted her to be my ma again. The way she had been, so long ago. When I could depend on everything she told me and I knew it was the truth.

'How could anyone know for sure?' she said. 'Sometimes I doubt that there's any surface up there at all any more. I know there once was, because I lived there. I see pictures of the past on my own walls, projected straight out of my brain. But then I get to wondering … what if I'm just making them up? What if I've been sitting here always in this room? What if I've invented it all?'

'But I'm here, Ma! I was there with you. We all lived together in our lovely Homestead…'

She looked at me. So sadly. 'But how do I know you're really here, and really being you, Lora? And how do you know for sure that I am who you think I am?'

'Oh, Ma … don't say that…'

She drifted over to a dispenser in the wall and pressed a button. She filled her palm with pale blue pills. 'These are good. Take some.'

I wouldn't.

'You shouldn't take everything at face value, Lora.'

'I don't!'

Ma shrugged. 'Don't believe everything you see and hear. I find it's best to keep yourself to yourself…'

I left her then. I felt sick deep down in my stomach.

Either she was going crazy, or she had a good point. And now I didn't know what to think or believe.

In the glowing corridor outside her room some of the Ancients were waiting for me. They brushed their silken fingers against my arms as I passed and called out to me.

I was in no mood for them, though. They always acted so gentle and they whispered so calmly, but I wasn't so sure they were as peaceful as I'd thought now. They surely intended us no good, the way they had us all doubting each other like this. It was their doing. It was like they were experimenting on us or something.

'Get your hands off me,' I told them.

'Lora,' one of them said. It was Arnold, the smallest one, who had come for me earlier. Now he was wearing a kind of cherubic expression. For some reason this Ancient was drawn to me in particular.

'You're the only one who's anywhere near friendly,' I told him again. 'The rest just pretend to be.'

'We aren't used to people like you,' the Ancient beamed at me, taking my hand in his.

'I'm not sure Arnold is the right name for you,' I told him. 'You don't really look like an Arnold.'

'I've never had a name before.' He shrugged. 'Arnold. I like it.'

'Humans like it when everyone has a proper name.'

'I see,' he smiled.

'Where are we going now?'

'I will take you to Peter. He has his own room now.'

Minutes later I found Peter in his own luxury den,

looking right at home, just like Ma and Hannah. He was hooked up with the same machines and gizmos.

Wouldn't you believe it, but Karl the cat-dog had his own comfy little podium too and he seemed blissed out, nibbling at some kind of pet chow.

'Peter, we've got to leave,' I told him. 'We've got to get Ma and Hannah out of here before they go completely out of their minds.'

His eyes were wide. He looked like someone who'd just been told the true meaning of existence. Right when he was least expecting it. His face was wide open with shock. 'I've got a magic picture,' he said. 'And it can show you other times and places.'

'Yeah,' I said. 'I've already had the demonstration from Hannah. And what I saw is the reason we gotta hit the road.'

Now he was looking at me funny.

Uh-oh, I thought. Here's another one who's getting stuck in the grip of the machinery.

'But can't we stay just a little longer, Lora? It's so peaceful here, and wonderful. And they've been so sweet to us ... and generous. Surely we deserve a little rest?'

Peter smiled at me and I thought: I've already lost him. He's well and truly caught.

Because that's what it was, to me. There was no doubt in my mind about what this whole place was.

A trap.

As I said, our rooms were arranged like cells in a honeycomb and all the floors were gently sloping, so there were no stairs or ladders. Just an endless parade of little rooms with obscure figures crouching in their own space.

The air was sweet like honey, too. Sometimes it was so sweet it was kind of sickening and I began to suspect that they were drugging us with something chemical. Some nauseating kind of stuff was getting into our heads and making them spin.

Even I wasn't thinking straight after several days down in the realm of the Ancients.

I sat stewing in the room they gave me.

I was furious with them all, with Ma and Hannah, and Peter and even Toaster, who had a room of his own as well. He claimed he was checking out their memory banks, but I reckoned he was just enjoying himself now.

I was feeling pretty much alone with my determination to break out of that dump and go back to save Da.

We'd come all this way for Ma and Hannah and they didn't even care. They just wanted to stay here.

Well, let them.

But it wasn't really them talking, was it? They were drugged up to the eyeballs. Their senses were stuffed and suffused by the input from all those speakers and screens in their rooms.

Speaking of which, I was refusing everything.

In my room the screens kept suggesting themselves and

blinking on and off all around me, promising to show me things. To distract me. To absorb me. To take up all my hours.

But I jammed my eyes shut and put my palms over my ears and sang out loud in my tuneless voice. They weren't gonna brainwash me as well.

Sometimes I'd sneak a little look.

I'd see pictures of the scarlet desert that we had crossed to get here. I saw our hefty lizards, Molly and George, waiting at the oasis where we'd left them, growing skinnier and more worried as the days went by. I saw that old Professor Swiftnick, who was once such an enemy and who had become a kind of friend – or at least, a companion on our journey.

Was it really him, or was it another illusion, as Ma had claimed? I saw him making his way back to the City Inside, with Barbra, the Servo from his precious Saucer craft. They were inching across the surface of the world, sending hopeful messages out ahead that they were returning from the wilderness.

Could any of these pictures be true?

Ma spent her days looking at pictures.

She had images plastered all over her walls, of life as it was in our Homestead. I sat with her sometimes and watched these memories flickering by.

We didn't talk much. She didn't want to hear what I had to say about leaving this place.

'No one ever leaves here,' she said.

'They can't keep us…' I glowered mutinously.

After several days in the Underworld I had lost all my bearings and sense of direction. I hardly knew which way was up or down.

I would never be able to find the elevator again, or know how to make it return me to Ma Taproot's tree.

If only I could contact her. Or Grandma, or anyone.

Could I send a message out of this place? If we could see pictures from outside – if any of those pictures were real – then maybe the signal could be reversed, and we could send pictures *out* into the world?

Toaster would know. He would be able to help, surely. But Toaster was swimming in the accumulated stores of knowledge. He lay in his room and sighed happily, and nothing I could say would wake him.

The sunbed was floating in bliss.

'Ma, Ma… Do you realise we're prisoners here?'

'What? Lora, don't be ridiculous. They're our friends. You mustn't be ungrateful to our hosts.'

'I try to be polite. But this place isn't for me. I can't sit in a little room forever staring at the walls. And Da is sick. It was no illusion. I know I have to get back and help him. We should never have left him alone in the City. We were caught up in the adventure of it all, boarding that Saucer. We were forced into it by the Authorities of the City Inside…'

She laughed. 'More wild talk of your faraway City! Did

you tell the Ancients all about it? They would be amazed to hear your tales of green glass towers and parties in planetaria…'

'Listen, Ma! Listen! They won't let me go. They won't let any of us go. We're stuck here forever, Ma. There is no way out that they're ever gonna show us.'

Ma tore her eyes away from her magic pictures and stared at me. 'Why … that's all right though, isn't it, Lora? We aren't unhappy. We aren't uncomfortable. We aren't in any danger or pain, are we? What could be nicer than living here?'

I left her and I was feeling angrier than ever.

Each day down here was an endless round of visiting my family and friends, and each visit made me more furious than the last.

As I was heading back to my own cell I heard small, squeaking footsteps behind me. I realised that someone was rushing after me along the smooth corridor.

It was someone I was ashamed to realise I had forgotten clean about in recent days.

'Watt!'

I was so pleased to see that little lampstand dashing up to me.

'I am Watt! Watt I am!'

He shone brilliantly, clicking his switch several times in succession, and I was scared he was gonna fuse himself in his excitement. 'Let me tell you! I have to tell you!'

'Calm down,' I told him. 'Come back to my cell. Tell me there. Where have you been? I thought we'd lost you…'

The truth was, the small Servo had dropped right out of my thoughts. Maybe it was an effect of the sweetness lacing the air, I dunno. But I hadn't thought about him once.

'They never gave me my own room,' he told me, as we hurried to my place. 'I guess you assumed I was sitting in my own cell, like the others, just pleasing myself and watching the screens. But I'm too insignificant, it turns out! They never thought I was worthy of my own room!'

'Oh, Watt – that's terrible! So, where have you been?' We reached my door; a wave of my hand unlocked it and I ushered him in.

'That's just the thing. I was free, you see, because I had no place. I was free to wander about unchecked in the realm of the Ancient Ones. No one took any notice of me. And Lora – the things I found! The things Watt found are incredible! I am Watt! Watt I found!'

'Calm down … tell me. What was it? What did you find?'

He flashed his bulb several times until the tiny filament burned and fizzed. 'I will tell you, Lora Robinson. I will tell you *who* I found, not what. She wasn't a Watt. She was a *Who!*'

'Then, who?' I said, trying not to lose my patience with him.

'She is a prisoner here, like the rest of us.' Watt grinned at me. 'Lora, I found Sook. *Sook is here.*'

13

'Tell me,' I told Watt.

He dimmed his bulb to conserve his energy and sat quite placidly while he told me his tale.

'As you know, the Ancients gave each of you a room and they separated you.'

My pulse was beating hard in my throat. I thought I knew where this story was leading. But how could it be? How could any of this be?

'I observed and I listened. I wandered around these endless corridors. And they really are endless, Lora. Watt has a good sense of direction, but he couldn't find his way out of here. I could never find the way back to the surface from here.'

'Tell me what you saw, and what you heard.'

'I heard crying. At first I thought it was a human voice. But I listened hard and followed the sobbing noise and I thought: that isn't human. Is it one of the Ancients? But I couldn't imagine one of them crying like that. It was husky and desperate. A smoky, powdery, crumbly voice. All disappointment and fear. And the Ancients are always smiling, aren't they? They're always so happy and pleased with themselves.'

'They certainly are.'

'I tracked down the noise and I poked my way into narrow corridors. There are smaller cells and smaller pockets of darkness in this honeycomb, you see. And only someone as small as me can slip between the translucent walls. One who comes with his own light source, such as I! I went exploring … and I squeezed into dark nooks and crannies of this Underworld … and eventually I found her.'

He paused dramatically, and clicked his light for emphasis.

'*Sook*?' I said. 'It was really her? How would you even know her? You've never met her before.'

'Of course, I didn't know who she was, or her importance to you, at first. All I saw was a girl with purple skin. She was slumped in golden chains in a tiny room.'

'Chains?' I was feeling sick by now.

'Oh, yes. She's chained to the wall in that dark little place. She was crying because of the pain and frustration because she'd tried to wrench herself free and her wrists were bleeding. Her wings were hurting her too. They are tattered and charred, you know. And when I saw them I knew what she was. She is a Martian Ghost, isn't she? One of the creatures that Thomas, your uncle, so fears. But you don't, do you? She was your friend. And when I talked to her, I thought: I wished she was my friend, too. She is strong and clever and proud. But she isn't well, Lora. She has been a prisoner here for too long. They aren't looking after her properly.'

I was on my feet, pacing furiously around my room. 'I knew it. I knew that they meant us harm. I knew all this nicey-nicey stuff was just a sham. Our own special rooms. Living in the lap of luxury. All this useless technology. Who cares about all that stuff? How can they treat Sook like this? What has she ever done to them?'

'They hate and fear her, the Ancients. They resent all the Martian Ghosts. They have destroyed many of them. Burned their wings and crisped their bodies into cinders. They have invaded their minds and driven them insane. I think that's why the Martian Ghosts laugh – some of them – the way they do. Heeeee heeeeee heeeee. Have you heard them laughing like that, Lora?'

I nodded. 'Yes. I used to think it was a horrible noise. I thought it was sinister. But I've learned since … I think that it's just how they breathe. And we did it to them, Watt. When we altered the climate on Mars. We made them breathe like that.'

Watt looked at me very seriously. 'I didn't know that. I thought they were just laughing like crazy people. Taunting everyone as they flew about. Thomas and my people would hunt them. He thought they were evil.'

'So did my folk in Our Town,' I said. 'But it was Sook who taught me different. Some of the Martian Ghosts are crazy, sure. But they aren't evil.'

Watt clicked at his light switch excitedly. 'Yes! Crazy! Many of the ghosts who fly too close to this place are driven crazy. But still they are driven on by their shared desire to keep people away from this place and from the Ancients. All they've ever wanted to do is to warn you humans. Keep away from the Ancients, Lora. Keep away from the very heart of Mars.'

'Yeah, well,' I said, croaking through a dry throat, very disturbed. 'I don't want to stay here a moment longer than we have to.'

'Sook has been a thorn in their Ancient flesh. They are treating her cruelly because she tried so hard to help you. She was a friend of yours. She told me about your history together. How you flew over the prairies and the mountains together.' Watt sighed happily. 'She told me all of this. It sounds like you shared some wonderful times.'

'We did! And she did save us; it's true. She couldn't tell me everything that was going on. But she did try to warn me. And she was treated badly by the City Insiders, too. Everywhere she's gone, she's been treated badly. Oh, will you take me to her, Watt? Right now? I've got to see her. Can you show me the way?'

'The way is too narrow,' he said. 'Only Watt can squeeze through. She is well-hidden and tucked away.'

'Then what can we do? How can we get her out? I've got to help her. I owe her so much…'

Watt considered the quandary for a few moments. 'Your friend Toaster is very strong. Those arms of his can heft anything. We will need his help to rescue Sook.'

'Great! Brilliant,' I said, knowing that Toaster would do anything I asked him.

But as things worked out, it wasn't going to be as easy as that.

I hadn't appreciated how brilliant Watt was.

Somehow he had kept tabs on where all of my friends were to be found in the bewildering maze of the Ancients. He led us swiftly through the labyrinth first to Peter's room, and then Toaster's.

We didn't rush. We didn't want to alert any of the Ancients to the fact that we were on a mission. When we passed any of the creatures we smiled and nodded happily. Doing our best to seem as if we hadn't a care in the world.

All the while I couldn't stop the thought drumming through my head: Sook was *here*.

She was trapped here with the rest of us. By the sound of it, she was in danger and in pain. I hated to think of her sobbing, alone, in some dark corner of this place.

'Lora!' Peter was surprised to see me. And there was something else. Was he irked, just a bit, to be interrupted?

Karl was jumping up at my legs and barking his head off.

'I need your help, Peter,' I told him. 'We've got a rescue mission. You'll…' Then I stopped and looked at what he was wearing. He was in one of the same dull coveralls that Ma had been wearing. His hair had been cut off, too. All those long locks of his, hacked down to nothing. 'You've settled in here, same as Ma and Hannah,' I said.

'What?' He frowned and looked down at his clothes. 'No Lora, that's just me pretending to fit in. It throws them off the scent if you go along with them a bit.' He smirked at me. 'I guess you never learned that ploy, did you? You just start complaining, as soon as you realise something isn't quite right?'

I stared at his pale, intelligent face. It was like he was disappointed in me. He looked as if he had had some time away from me, and realised that he was fed up with the way I behaved and lived my life. In many ways he had a point. I was hopeless at trying to fit in with anything new. And I couldn't pretend to be happy, like the rest of them seemingly could. But that was just me, and he was my friend, wasn't he?

'Watt has found Sook,' I announced. I didn't see the point in wasting any more time. 'We have to rescue her. She's chained up. They've burned her wings to tatters.'

'Sook?' he frowned. 'Oh, your friend. Who no one else has ever really, properly met. I remember.'

'We'll get Toaster next,' I continued. 'He's strong enough to break through to where she's being held…'

'Lora, look,' Peter interrupted. 'Before you go haring off and dragging us all with you. There's something you have to see. Since we've been here, I've been experimenting with these screens…' He waved one hand and a whole wall of magic pictures opened up like eyes.

'Yes, I know all about them,' I said. 'Hannah and Ma are obsessed with them. They stare at the pictures all day long.'

'I am Watt,' Watt said shrilly. 'They never gave me a room of my own. I've never seen the pictures. I'd like to see them, if I may.'

Peter smiled at him, and suddenly there was the warmth in my friend's expression that I'd been missing.

For a few minutes I'd been thinking he'd become distant from me, and that I'd lost him, perhaps through some stupid fault of my own. I was relieved to see a sign of the Peter I had come to know through our adventures together. That smile of his brought us closer in a flash.

'Take a look, Watt,' Peter said, and expertly clenched his fingers and seemed to focus his thoughts with a frown. He'd really picked up the knack for controlling the pictures, it seemed.

And all at once we saw a view of the baking dunes of the Martian desert. Crimson hills retreated into a hazy distance and, in the foreground, two bulky figures were stumbling clumsily. The picture became clearer all at once, and we saw the burly figure of Professor Swiftnick in his green tailcoat and tattered cravat, and the oblong form of Barbra, his vending machine.

They were on their last legs, exhausted by the desert winds and heat.

But there was a ship sailing through the sands towards them. It came from the direction of the green translucent dome on the horizon. An airship with papery sails, gliding smoothly, twenty feet above the shifting sands. It looked magnificent.

We watched the man and the Servo jumping for joy as they realised they were about to be rescued.

'I'm glad they got back home,' I said. 'It's good to know.'

'Who is that wonderful Servo?' Watt cried out, his light bulb flickering excitedly. 'She is *incredible*! Look how she is carrying him, those final few yards, as the ship approaches. What dedication! And what a delectable outer shell she wears! Who is she? What is she?'

Peter chuckled. 'That's Barbra the vending machine. You'd like her in person, Watt. We all do. But Lora, listen. I was tuned into them earlier too, a few hours ago. The picture was showing this same view. With the sailing ship approaching them, and their rescue and being taken back to the City Inside. But at one point Karl here became so excited at seeing Barbra again, he barked loudly at her, as if to draw her attention.'

Even now Karl was in my arms, wriggling excitedly as he watched events on the screen. 'So?'

'He barked pretty loudly. You know how piercing his racket can be,' said Peter, ruefully. 'And this is the amazing bit, Lora. Barbra, up there on the picture, turned round and looked straight at us. She *heard* him, Lora. She actually heard him barking, across all that distance.'

'You're joking…!'

But he wasn't. 'Karl. Come over here. Do it again!'

The little cat-dog was only too glad to be of help. He bounded out of my arms and sat on the console. Then, on Peter's command, he let out a volley of his shrillest barks.

Barbra the vending machine was filling up the screen again.

'Look! She's doing it again!' shouted Peter, over the racket. 'She's turning and looking at us again! Just like before!'

More than that. This time Barbra had clearly heard the barking because she even said, 'Karl?'

We heard her!

Peter leapt out a whoop of joy, and Karl barked even louder.

Professor Swiftnick shouted at her, gaining her attention again. 'Barbra! Stop daydreaming!' And together they carried on waving at their rescue ship.

'We've lost her attention…' I said.

Peter was grinning at me, jubilant at proving his point. 'But you see, don't you, Lora? Don't you see what this means?'

My eyes were wide with amazement. 'They can *hear* us. We can see and hear them, all the way across the other side of Mars. And they can hear us, too. Sometimes. Somehow.' But I shook my head, confused. 'But … the pictures aren't happening live, are they? You said yourself that you've seen this rescue before…'

146

'That's right. I don't know how it works. But it's … telepathic somehow. It's a deep connection between people, all that distance apart. We can replay scenes and somehow interact with them. I feel that this is the truth, Lora. These magic pictures aren't just one-way. They aren't just some kind of soporific entertainment allowing us to watch but not take part in the world…'

'We can send messages!' I burst out happily. 'I think you're right, Peter. I hope you're right.' I hugged him hard. I knew I could depend on him. I should have known he'd have figured out something clever before too long.

Watt gave a discreet cough. 'I think we'd better get on with our mission. Who knows if the Ancients are aware of the things we're learning, and the plans we're brewing. I am Watt! I have a rescue to carry out! We must carry on!'

'He's right,' said Peter. 'We have to assume that the Ancients have magic pictures of their own. At any moment, should they choose to, they could tune in and see what we're doing…'

I nodded. 'Good point. Let's get Toaster out of his cell. We must hurry. I just hope we can drag him out of his precious sea of knowledge…'

14

Toaster didn't need telling twice.

'Toaster? Something's up,' I told him gently.

There were wires and tubes and electrodes hooking him up to the machinery in his room. His entire body was shimmering and pulsing with golden light. But at the sound of my voice he sat up immediately.

He knew something important was up this time. He heard the urgency in my voice and, as always for our family, he was happy to put aside his own desires. And so he came swimming back from the depths of the Ancients' memory banks.

I quickly told him what we must do.

'I understand,' he nodded solemnly, knowing he was the strongest in our group. He seemed shocked that Sook was here in the Underworld and that, according to Watt, she was being treated as a prisoner. He had met Sook before and knew her importance to me. True, their meeting had been a strange affair: it had been the day when Sook had taken hold of our hands and flown my brother, me and our sunbed all the way to the City Inside ... and it had seemed to happen in a kind of dream....

Watt led us through the labyrinth. Deeper and deeper, until none of us – not even Toaster – could have found our way back out again.

'Strange we haven't seen any of the Ancients,' Peter murmured.

The air was heavier and darker. No longer clear but with an amber colour to it.

There were cells here, just like ours. But they had a look of neglect about them. It was as if they hadn't been lived in for a long time.

Watt was inquisitive as ever, stopping at doors and heaving them open. 'Look in here,' he said solemnly.

'What?'

Inside this particular room, just one of many in that corridor, was some sort of control desk, a screen, and a chair similar to those in the rooms we had been given.

Peter and Toaster joined me in the doorway when they heard my stifled cry of shock.

'It's…' began Peter, but he couldn't even say the word.

'A dead human being,' said Toaster.

'It's someone who's been here a long time,' I said. 'It's like a skeleton lying there.'

Watt was pushing open other doors along that stretch of corridor. 'Don't look in these. They're all the same. Everyone in this area is dead. They've wasted away to nothing.' His voice was hushed and horrified.

I looked at Toaster and Peter. 'Do you see what they do now? This is what becomes of people down here.'

Peter looked shocked to his core. 'You were right, Lora. They hook us to their machinery and they just … suck all of the life out of us.'

I nodded. 'I can hardly believe what we're looking at myself. But I just knew. I knew something wasn't right.'

'Maybe they don't think about individuals in the same way we do,' said Peter slowly, as if he was trying to work it out. 'I don't think death means the same to them. They don't understand it… One person's death isn't as important to them as it is to us perhaps…'

Watt clicked his light to get our attention. 'We must keep moving. They won't want us down here, learning their secrets. We must go on.'

He was right. We started moving at a quicker pace.

This deep in the honeycomb the sweetness was even worse, and I felt thick-headed as I turned to look at Peter. Karl was in his arms, shivering with alarm.

What was I doing to my friends? Leading them into danger? Making them betray their new hosts in this Underworld paradise? Their lives – all our lives – could be so much easier if we simply gave up and stayed inside our luxurious cells. If we abandoned our notions of freedom and enjoyed the machinery and the magic pictures we were provided with, perhaps we could even be happy…

I shook my head to clear it of this nonsense. The Ancients and their ideas were creeping into my thoughts.

I had seen those bodies. We all had. We knew what became of people who gave in and stayed in their rooms.

It was a relief when Watt stopped suddenly and pointed to a very small gap in the wall, no higher than my knees.

Toaster hurried forward, placing his clamp-like hands on the walls. 'The very substance of this place is living matter,' he told us. 'I have learned a lot about it already ... and really, the whole of this Underworld is a kind of living being ... the very walls are a fleshy, membranous substance.'

This creeped me out, to be honest. I didn't like to think that we were prisoners inside something alive and, possibly, even intelligent.

'I sense that Watt is correct,' Toaster continued. 'Sook is back there somewhere. I just need to persuade these walls to move apart fractionally...'

Toaster seemed to go into a trance.

Peter gave me a quizzical look, as if he was doubting our sunbed, but I knew better than that. If Toaster claimed he could do a thing, then no doubt he could.

In truth, all I could think about was seeing Sook again. Here she was, after all this time. I thought I'd only ever hear her voice in my head, and never be sure whether it was real or imaginary.

'The walls are moving!' Watt gasped. 'He's doing it! I thought he'd have to use brute strength ... but somehow he's *persuading* the walls to move!' The small Servo was looking up at Toaster, glimmering with hero worship.

'Hurry,' Toaster told us. 'Go and talk with Sook. I will keep the walls apart … but I can only do so for so long. You must come back when I call, otherwise you will be trapped. Also, be aware that the Ancients are linked to the very fabric of their city. They will know what we are doing. They will come to stop us. So be quick, Lora.'

'I will.'

Watt flicked on his bulb and led the way into the still-narrow corridor that Toaster had created.

I had to crouch and squirm along behind him, ducking and holding in my panic at the closeness of the walls.

'Good luck,' Peter said, and Karl gave a supportive yip.

Then I was in the dimly lit tunnel, which squeezed closer and closer and almost sealed itself up again as we passed through. I felt like I was being eaten up and swallowed. As I trod grimly onwards, all I could see to concentrate on was little Watt, who bravely plunged ahead.

'Not far! This way!' he kept saying. 'I've been this way before, and I know! I am Watt! I know the way!'

I thought again how I'd been right to trust my instincts, letting the lampstand join our team when he did. He had been the one to help us find the Underworld and now he had showed he had another crucial role to play, and this was it. He was taking me to Sook.

'And here she is,' said the small lamp happily, as the soft corridor widened into a dark chamber and his light bulb flared.

I staggered into the opening and almost fell on my knees. It was such a relief to be out of the squashy tunnel.

There she was, slumped against the dark orange wall, held in golden shackles.

'Oh, Sook! It really is you! You're here!'

She looked terrible. Waif-like and skinny. I could hardly see her magnificent wings. They were crumpled beneath her like an old ragged blanket. She was a broken puppet, hanging in a tangle of useless strings. Could she even hear me?

'Sook, Sook … it's me, Lora. We've found you! Watt here led me to you. Can you believe it?'

Watt was glowing with pride, but he didn't waste any more time. He dashed over to Sook, and made his bulb grow brighter, to illuminate our reunion, but he was also attempting to burn through the resinous stuff her chains were made out of. They smouldered at the heat of his bulb. 'I can do it! Watt can do it!'

'L-Lora?'

My friend's eyes were open and they were staring at me. Lilac and spiralling. Brilliant and mysterious as they ever were.

She didn't question what I was doing there, or how I had found her. She didn't even look particularly amazed that I was here: down in the depths of the Underworld of the Ancients. Sook and I were used to seeing each other in the strangest of places and at the most unexpected times.

'I'm so happy to see you, Lora,' she said. And her voice

was gaspy and rough. She sounded a hundred years older than when I'd seen her last. It was like most of the life had been dragged out of her.

'I'm so happy to see you, too,' I said. 'It's wonderful. I never thought I would…'

Her eyes narrowed and she cut through my gabbling. 'But this is the *worst* place for you to be, Lora. This is the one place I kept warning you never to come. The single most terrible place in our whole world. This is the heart of Mars. No one ever flies free from here.'

Looking back, we only had a few minutes together. Time was ticking loudly while I stood there, staring at her broken form.

Watt kept his light bulb trained on us, and back along that narrow corridor, Toaster was straining every mental and hydraulic muscle to hold the way open for our return. And somewhere in the corridor beyond Peter and Karl were keeping their eyes peeled for the Ancient Ones.

But for a few moments we were caught in a shadowy bubble of time: me and Sook.

For a tiny interlude it was just like it had always been between us.

Everything else stopped.

We were just two girls from entirely different species, and we had so much to tell each other we hardly knew where to start.

I could have wept when I saw her shattered wings tremble and stir, as if they were longing to spread out so she could take to the air.

'I came here looking for my mother and sister,' I told her. 'I didn't know you were here. Look, we can get you out of this place. Watt, can you smash those chains? We can escape...'

'There's no escape from the Ancient Ones,' Sook shook her head. 'Too many of my kind have been taken prisoner. They don't let us go again. They trap us here and gradually absorb all our life force. Everything that is ours becomes theirs.'

'I won't let them do this to you...'

'They've already taken a lot out of me,' Sook whispered. 'I won't leave this place now. But you, Lora. You *must* get out. You need to get out *now*. The things they do to human beings are, I believe, even worse. That's why we were warning you, all of you humans, to leave this part of Mars. It's why the City Inside was safer...'

'W-what do they do to human beings?' I asked. At last, I thought. Answers at last.

'They want your minds, Lora. They have some strange ideas about the human mind. They think you all know magical things. They believe you have knowledge that they crave...'

I stared at her, uncomprehending. 'What knowledge? What could any of us know that creatures as powerful as the Ancients didn't already know?'

Sook started coughing, her face was looking strained and exhausted. Watt threw down the golden chains with a clatter. 'I can't do it! Watt can't break them! They're strong! So strong!'

'Sook? We don't know anything … we have no special knowledge…'

Sook's lilac eyes were glittering with tears when she looked up at me again. 'You had Starships, Lora. You people came here, to our world, on board Starships that floated through the void. Can't you see? You take all that for granted. But can't you see that, to anyone on Mars who'd never seen such things before … that was like the most amazing magic?'

'But … but … that wasn't *us*…' I said. 'That was our grandparents. And even our grandparents didn't build the ships. They didn't even fly them. Only very few of us knew how the Starships actually worked…'

Sook coughed, she couldn't catch her breath. 'Ah, but all minds are linked, aren't they? What one knows, you all know. That's how things work on Mars. All the Ancients share the same mind, the same heart. We Martian Ghosts are the same. That is how I know, for example, that my father is dead. Because I no longer hear his faraway thoughts in my head. And I know, Lora, that you were there with him in some of his last moments, and I'm grateful for your kindness. All sentient beings are linked by their minds and their spirits. That's what the Ancients believe.'

This was too much for me to take in. I was distracted

for a few seconds, thinking of Sook's father when we found him lying in that ruined house. He had coughed just like Sook was doing now, and that made me scared that she was about to die as well.

I shook my head to clear away these terrible thoughts and suddenly I realised: the Ancient Ones had got it all wrong. They assumed human beings are linked telepathically, like they are. They believed we live inside each other's thoughts.

But we truly don't, do we?

We're all so separate in our minds.

All of us live so far apart, alone in our own skulls.

We aren't like Martians at all.

'Lora!' There was a shout behind, from deep in the small tunnel. It was Toaster's booming voice. 'I can't hold this open much longer. You must leave … *now!*'

I stared desperately at Sook. 'I want to take you with me.'

Watt looked alarmed. 'I can't free her. Watt has tried! It's hopeless! I can't break these terrible chains…'

'We'll get you out!' I was crying now. My voice was thick and strangulated and I was shouting. 'We will, Sook. I don't care what we have to do. Anything! But you're coming with us. I won't leave you here!'

There were more shouts from Toaster. Now his voice was joined by Peter's, further away. He sounded panicked. Something was going on. Something awful.

'Lora, listen to me,' said Sook.

She was being too calm and determined.

I guessed what she was going to say, and I didn't like it.

'Lora, you have to leave me here. You can't free me from this trap. My wings are ruined, anyway, and my limbs are too weak. I'd only ever hold you up. You know that. If the rest of you are to stand any chance at all you must leave me here. You must go! Now!'

Even as she said this I felt sure she didn't really mean it. She hadn't given up hope completely. Her wings were betraying her, right in that moment. They were buzzing and trembling against the shadowy walls as if they were using the last of their strength in trying to break free.

'Watt believes she is right, Lora,' said the little lamp. 'If we stay here much longer, the corridor will collapse and I do not know if another way out can be found…'

'I won't leave you, Sook.'

'Lora, you must,' said Sook. 'Look at me. Look into my eyes.'

'Sook … I…'

'I know,' she smiled.

That wide, lipless mouth of hers opened in a gentle smile. I stared at her tiny, pointed teeth.

She was so different, so alien.

And yet I loved her.

I had loved her since that first night she folded me up into her strong, slender arms and we flew into the brilliant night above the prairie.

'I know, Lora. And because we love each other I refuse to let you stay here with me, lost in the depths of this terrible place. You have amazing things to do with your life. You have no idea how much you will do, and where your life can take you.' She chuckled as she coughed. 'Heeeee. I'm spooky, remember? I can tune in to strange vibrations. I can sense a little of the future. And I know … I'm telling you … you have an incredible future. Your life has barely started. And I must stay behind. Heeeee heeeeee. My place is here. I must stay at this point in your story. I must be content with the part I have been allowed to play.

'And I love you, too, Lora. But now we must part. And you have to leave me here. Heeeee heeeeee heeeee.

'Now, go! Run! Before Toaster's strength gives out.'

I stood there, frozen. 'I … I can't go, Sook…'

'You must, Lora. Now the Ancients are coming. You must protect your friends from them. You must go right now. Goodbye, my Lora.'

And I knew she was right.

I kissed her.

And then I turned to run.

15

I didn't look back.

I kept my head down and I pushed forward as fast as I could. But the walls were squeezing closer the whole time. The soft, translucent walls were pressing in on me.

I heard Toaster crying out, his voice booming through the dark air: 'Lora! Lora, you must leave her! Before it's too late!'

My head was pounding and my tongue was thick in my throat. Suddenly there was noise and confusion. All I could think about was Sook's face.

I knew I had seen it for the very last time.

I had abandoned her.

I was forced onto my hands and knees by the tunnel walls squashing so close together. I could feel them straining and pushing closer, and I knew that Toaster was doing his best, but I wasn't sure it was going to be enough.

I heard Watt's shrill voice, urging me on from behind. I was aware of his flickering glow in the gloom as he screeched: 'Keep moving, Lora! I am here! I am Watt! I am right behind you!'

It seemed to take several decades to make my way through that horrible corridor.

When I eventually emerged into the lighter, brighter expanse beyond I almost wished I hadn't made it.

Toaster was on the point of collapse.

As soon as he saw that I was safe he stepped away from the aperture. His whole metallic frame was shaking. His limbs were vibrating with all the power he could muster. Smoke was seeping out of his joints and the cracks in his glass panels.

He gave a great cry of robotic pain, and suddenly all his efforts ceased.

The hole in the wall behind me disappeared at once.

I was far across the corridor. I'd flung myself there, balling up all my strength and bravery. I was safe. I was free.

But when I turned back to see the closed-up wall I'd just passed through, I saw that I was alone.

'No…!' I cried out. 'Watt was behind me!' I yelled. 'Where is he?'

Toaster stared at me, dumbfounded and with no strength left. 'I did my best…' he intoned.

'But it wasn't good enough,' I yelled. 'Not for Watt. He's in there. Open it up again! Get him out!'

But the wall was smooth and featureless once more.

There was nothing to say where that doorway had been.

There was no way back to Watt and Sook. They were lost somewhere, deep inside the honeycomb.

Now Peter was standing beside me, helping me to my feet, while Karl barked and jumped at me.

'Peter, Watt is stuck in there. We've left him behind. He might have been crushed...'

'I know, I know,' Peter whispered, hugging me hard. He was trembling. 'I'm just glad you're safe, Lora. We could have lost you, too. You could have been killed.'

I pulled myself away from him. 'I don't care about that. What about that little Servo? All he ever did was help us. He's gone now. We let him down. He gave up his little life...'

Toaster took a step towards me. 'He did it willingly. He died in your service, Lora. He gave you his allegiance and this was his duty...'

I turned on Toaster then. I couldn't help it. 'You could have saved him. He was right behind me. All you had to do was keep that tunnel open just a few seconds longer. He could have made it ... but he wasn't worth it, was he? He was just a little robot. He was nothing to you.'

'Lora,' Peter tried to stop me. 'Toaster tried his best. He just about tore himself apart keeping that tunnel open as long as he could...'

'It wasn't enough,' I said, crying. 'It just wasn't long enough. I needed longer ... I could have freed Sook. I could have brought her out and saved her. Instead ... instead ... she's lost. And Watt is lost. Or they're both dead. I don't know.'

'You saw Sook? You talked to her?' Peter asked.

I never had time to tell him anything about our meeting. Suddenly Toaster was pushing past and silencing us. 'They're here. They've found us.' His voice was very flat.

'Who have?' said Peter, but we all knew who Toaster meant.

Everything went quiet. Unnaturally quiet.

Then we could hear them coming after us.

The slither, scrape, shuffle of them.

The Ancients were making their gradual way towards us. They didn't have to hurry. They knew we were lost in their labyrinth.

We had been foolish to think we could move around and run about at our leisure. We were idiots to think we could poke holes in their world and rescue each other and escape from this terrible place.

The truth was, we were caught in the domain of the Ancient Ones and we were utterly in their power.

They came crawling on their hands and knees because they had grown tall again. This was their world and they controlled everything here, and they wanted us to know that. Once more they seemed to have become huge, angelic beings with hidden fangs and claws that scraped on the fleshy floors and walls.

They moved slowly but surely, staring ahead, smiling in their gentle way. Their eyes were full of flickering golden flames.

And now they had us. They knew it and we knew it.

All the pretending and games were over now.

We had been offered their prizes and their rewards: their luxurious rooms and their magic pictures and we had refused them.

Or I had, at any rate. And I had encouraged my friends to spurn those gifts as well. We had been more intent on causing a fuss, on learning the truth and then on finding Sook.

Now the Ancients had come to find us, shifting forms as they did so, extending their long, skinny fingers like talons and their dark eyes filling up with golden flames.

'We have been watching you, and you are most interesting,' the first one said. There were three of them. They still gazed at us with gentle faces. They were like smooth-faced old people. All the wrinkles soothed away. All the wisdom still there, somehow. Their voices were very soft, but somehow they were all the more terrifying for that.

'Most interesting, you are,' their leader went on. 'And are those tears you're shedding, little girl? For that Martian Ghost? And that broken Servo-Furnishing? Do you really regret their deaths?'

The word stabbed at me. 'Deaths?'

'Oh, they're assuredly dead. All of you are dead, when we will it to be true. Your lives are forfeit. Your only hope is to be useful to us.'

I shook my head. 'We won't do anything for you. We'd rather die.'

I felt Peter take my hand. At first I thought he was trying to quieten me, but I realised he was standing firm with me. I realised I depended on him being there at moments like this. He made me feel stronger in myself.

The Ancient Ones chuckled softly at us. The first one said, 'You'll do what we want. Come along. Come with us. It's time for us to tell you what we want you to do.'

First of all, they took us to Ma's room. She was absorbed in watching her pictures on the wall. I caught a glimpse of the red dust of the prairie, and images of burden beasts pulling a cart through a field of swaying blue corn. And was that Da, staring out from the tender stalks, straight back at her?

Suddenly Ma became aware that she had visitors. She looked round sharply.

'What's going on? What's happening here?'

What must we have looked like, I wondered? I was dishevelled, and Toaster was buckled and soot-stained, just like he used to be when he worked in the fields. All of us were doleful and defiant-looking.

The Ancients pushed us inside her room, smiling softly, like they always did, teeth hidden again, eyes black once more. They shrank themselves down in an instant so they could step inside and surround her.

'We want to see you altogether. Quite soon. You will wait for us here.'

'But … you have disturbed me!' Ma was very agitated. I saw her turn and fumble for a handful of her pills, which she quickly downed. 'I was watching something very important and interesting…'

The Ancients simply smiled at her, as if there was nothing they could do. They all looked at me with sorrowful expressions, as if explaining that I was the one responsible for all the upset. Then, soundlessly, they left us alone.

A long couch rose out of the fluid floor for me to lie on. I simply collapsed onto it. I was worn out from my ordeal in that awful place, and I was sick in my heart because of everything that had happened.

When I closed my eyes all I could see was Sook's anguished face. I could hear her strange, fluting voice inside my head, telling me to run away and get away and leave her.

And I could feel Watt's tiny hand in mine as he urged me to get away. The bright little filament of his bulb was burned into my retina when I squinched my eyes closed.

They were both gone forever. Maybe there was something I could have done to save them, but I hadn't.

I had lost them.

Peter was sitting beside me on the couch. He stroked my hair and tried to speak to me.

'It's all gonna be all right, Lora.'

'Is it? It's all my fault. What happened to Sook … and to Watt … it's all because of me.'

'No, it's not. You tried to save them…'

'I don't want to talk about it now.'

I wasn't in the mood to hear his denials. Wordlessly, Karl came creeping into my arms for a hug and I let him. His metal limbs were cool, but his body was very warm, trembling and purring as hard as he could in order to comfort me.

Ma was still muttering and complaining. Toaster plugged himself into her machines and I supposed he was surfing through the databanks once more. I heard Peter talking to him, and it sounded as if the two of them were conspiring over something.

Some time later the doors swished open and Hannah was shoved inside our cell with us. She seemed just as surprised and as annoyed as Ma had been, to have her seclusion spoiled.

'What's going on?' I heard her say, pertly. 'Ma, what's happening? Why's Lora here? And Toaster – is that really you? You look different! And these others? Who are they?' she sighed. 'Have they done something wrong? Are we all being punished because of them?'

Hannah was a bright kid. She always had been. She had worked out straight away that something was up, and I was at fault.

'I-I don't know what's happening,' Ma stammered. She had put an eye mask on, and was trying to act as if none of us were there. 'The Ancients brought them here, I don't know why. It's not like they don't have rooms of their own.'

Hannah said, 'We must have displeased them. One or more of us must have done something terrible. I know I haven't broken the rules. And I doubt, dear mother, that you have done anything wrong?'

'Me? How can I do anything wrong? All I do all day is sit here, watching the pictures…'

'Exactly. Then it must be Lora. Lora and her friends. Lora who's never happy.'

All right. That was enough. I wasn't going to lie there all day pretending to rest, listening to this. Whatever they'd done to change her, I had no patience with making allowances for that now. She had to snap back into being her natural self. She just had to.

I sat up and looked at her. 'Yeah, we did something that the Ancients are pretty mad about. And I guess they're holding the whole lot of us responsible. So that's just tough, Hannah. They'll probably never let you watch the picture show again. They'll probably take your rooms off you … forever.'

Okay, I know I had meant to taunt them both, but even I was taken aback by their reactions. Hannah gasped and Ma cried out, and started sobbing at once. I watched my sister fall into my mother's arms and start acting again like the baby I remembered her being. Soon they were wailing incoherently at the thought of being evicted.

I decided I would tell them about the bodies we had found. The cadavers in the abandoned rooms. If they said anything else about staying here and how wonderful it was, I reckoned it was time to tell them the truth.

Then Peter said, 'Lora, come and see this.'

I was glad of the distraction.

I hurried over to find that Toaster had raised a panel of delicate machinery from the hidden interior of the machine. Somehow he had wedged the whole thing open to reveal a mass of electronic circuits. They didn't look like the workings of any kind of machine I had ever seen, even in the sophisticated City Inside. The circuitry looked more like a living mass of insects, buzzing around in a nest: everything was moving and glinting and shifting about. Toaster was jabbing at the innards with a set of tools attached to his hand.

'What are you doing?' I asked. I hoped it was some kind of awful sabotage. I imagined our clever sunbed was getting himself into the workings of the Ancients' city. They were too dependent on their automated lifestyles and this was how he was going to prove it to them. Their bright, easy, peaceful lives were about to be disrupted: he was going to switch them off, perhaps...

'I've been wondering about this for days,' said Peter. The magic pictures work both ways, don't they? We all sensed that. Not only were we spying on people halfway across the world … we could make them hear us, too. We could perhaps, communicate with them…'

I thought of that queer moment when Barbra the vending machine had looked up, surprised, and seemed as if she was somehow hearing us. She looked as if she was hearing ghosts, and then seemed to dismiss the noise.

But it had been a big moment. It had proved something.

'I think we can do it,' Peter said. 'I think we can send a proper message. Toaster told me he can reverse the polarity of the machine. He thinks he knows how to get a message out…'

I yelped. 'That's why he was swimming in all that data! He wasn't just being selfish and drinking up the knowledge for the sake of it!' Excitedly I patted the sunbed's shining body. 'He was finding out how all this stuff works!'

'Exactly, Lora,' said Toaster stiffly. 'And I think I have the hang of it now…'

All at once the magic pictures in Ma's room were coming to life in full, glowing colour.

We had to shield our eyes for a moment or two; everything was so bright. Ma hugged Hannah closer to her. She looked affronted that someone else was controlling her pictures.

'Toaster can do most of it,' said Peter. 'But now we need you, Lora.'

I nodded. 'What do I need to do?'

'We've got to send a message out of here. We need to tell them we're being held prisoner.'

'B-but … who can I tell? Grandma? I can't tell Da … he's ill.' I racked my brains. I needed to tell someone about Da as well. I could save him and I could save us, perhaps, by sending a single message…

And all at once I knew who we needed to contact.

'Quickly,' Peter urged. 'Before the Ancients realise what we're doing with their precious machinery…'

'Al,' I said, making up my mind. 'We've got to contact Al. I'm sure he'll be able to help us. I'm certain he can.'

16

'Al…? Al, are you there? Can you hear me?'

I had been pretty close to my brother when we were younger. Where we grew up, in our Homestead on the prairie, the only other kids we ever saw were miles away in Our Town. We saw them maybe once a month. So Al and I were each other's best friends, kind of. We used to bicker and fight a lot. I guess I was tougher than he was. He'd come off worse when we'd tussle and Da would have to separate us.

But I was never in any doubt then that we were on the same side, always.

But it had been hard in recent times, ever since we arrived in the City Inside, to remember that we once had such a great connection. I dated all the changes to that moment when we'd first arrived in that green glass City and everything was so strange. We thought we'd be there forever and the place would turn us into completely new people.

Except I stayed the same. Al was the one who changed.

He was always better at fitting in than I was.

'*Al*…? It's Lora…'

His face was on all the screens in Ma's room: a close-up view so big we couldn't even see where he was, or if he was alone. This machinery was so weird, it could zoom in on the person who was half a world away and bring them almost too close to focus on.

I wondered, could he see us? Or just hear my voice? Was it inside his head, or would it be audible to anyone in the same room as him? Would he be able to dismiss my communication as just his imagination?

'Lora? It can't be you... What's happening? Where are you?'

He looked older as he squinched up his face. Then I thought: was I communicating with him now, this very moment? Or maybe this message was being transmitted through time and I was talking to a future Al, an older Al?

Ma and the others gathered around me, staring up at his face. Ma tried to catch his attention.

'Al, it's your mother! Can you hear me?'

Al's face grew even more puzzled. 'Lora, what's happening? Is that ... is that ... *Ma*?'

A great big grin cracked my face open. I sure hoped he could see it.

'It is, Al! Ma's here! And Hannah's here, too. We found them! We succeeded in our mission!'

He was dumbstruck. His mouth dropped open. I'd told him great news. The best news. So I'd give him a few moments to absorb that, and then I'd follow it up with the less-good news.

'You did it! My god, you did it!' His smile was like sunlight and Earth light pouring into Ma's small room. I realised how long it had been since any one of us had experienced unalloyed joy like this.

'But Al, Al, you've got to listen…'

'I can't believe it! I knew you were determined and everything … but when we watched that green Saucer take off part of me thought that we'd never see you again, Lora. I felt such a coward, staying behind.'

'Al, you've got to listen to me. I don't know how long I can keep this connection open. We're using this strange technology belonging to these people called the Ancient Ones, and they'll stop us any minute…'

But Al was still burbling on, happily, not really listening to me.

'And when they found Professor Swiftnick wandering in the desert with that robot … and brought him home by airship, well, I thought that was it. I thought that was definitely the last I'd hear from you.'

That brought me up short, although I'd seen this picture already. 'What's that about Swiftnick?'

Toaster leaned forward, his hands still on the intricate controls.

'And a robot, did he say? So what you saw on Peter's screen was right? Barbra really is safe as well?'

'Hey, Toaster!' Al hooted. 'I can hear you, too!' Then he looked abashed. 'Uh, I'm in a carriage on a Pipeline train right now. The other passengers all think I'm crazy. Let me go out into the corridor, where it's more private…'

We had to wait a couple of moments before he could talk with no one else listening in. I wondered what he must look like, addressing the empty air, like he was talking to phantoms.

'We saw Swiftnick made it back to the City, with Barbra,' I said. 'When did that happen?'

'Just last week. He was in all the press. Tillian interviewed him and I went along. I wanted to know about you but, my god, he's full of himself. All about how he survived the wicked wilderness, and the crashing of his precious skyship, and terrible monsters, and demonic trees … ruthless outlaws and everything. And … and how you lot were all most probably dead already. How you'd been sacrificed … to some kind of evil gods in the northern swamplands…'

'Ha! Not quite! Not yet!' I said. 'But that's a reasonably accurate summary of what went on…'

'He made himself out to be a real hero, of course.'

'I bet. Look, Al, we can't waste any more time. What about Da? What's happening to Da?'

He looked puzzled. 'I haven't seen him in a while. A few weeks. I guess he's busy… We've all been busy…'

I interrupted brusquely. This was important. 'He's sick.

I believe he's really sick. You need to go over there right now and see.'

'O-okay…' Al said. 'I'll go there today. I'll check on him. But how do you know what's going on with Da?'

'Trust me on this,' I said. 'I'm communicating with you through this machinery of the Ancients. We saw Da. He needs our help.'

Al looked confused. 'I … I want to believe it's all true. It seems so fantastic, though. Talking to you like this. And Ma … is it true? Is it really you?'

Ma looked at me before speaking. There was wonderment in her face. 'Will it work if I talk to him? Will he hear me?'

'He can hear me, can't he?'

She seemed nervous all of a sudden. Almost shy of speaking up. 'Al … are you really there in this City that Lora talks about?'

'I am! I am, Ma! And there's so much to tell you. So much has happened. I can't wait to see you again … It'll be soon, won't it? You'll all come here, won't you? Lora's gonna bring you to the City Inside…'

Ma looked hopeful for a second. There was a flicker of pure optimism on her face. She was hugging Hannah to her. Then both their faces became solemn.

'Honey, we'd love to. We thought this Insider City of yours was just Lora's imaginings. It's been hard to know what to believe here in the Underworld…'

'But it's all real, Ma! The City and everything!' Al was laughing.

The picture fizzed and fractured. Toaster's careful hands danced across the controls, but he was losing the connection, I could tell.

'It's all so real. And you'll … you'll all be here with us … the family… Our family… The Robinsons will be together again!'

As Al's picture started to break up completely Ma sighed and shook her head.

'I don't think so, son. I don't think I'm going to be leaving this place. I'm so sorry about that. But somehow I just don't think I ever will.'

I couldn't believe what I was hearing.

'Are you kidding, Ma? But we've come all this way looking for you! We risked everything coming down here…' I was staring at her, amazed.

But her face was closed up like a cupboard. Hannah was hugging her and glaring at me.

'Don't shout at her, Lora,' my sister snapped. 'You'll just upset her. She knows her mind. She knows what she wants.'

'But…!' I appealed to the others, to Toaster and Peter.

There was nothing they could do. Toaster had always been her servant and he couldn't start telling her what to do. Peter didn't know her at all.

I looked again at my mother and realised that now I

didn't know her, either. She hadn't been herself after Da had Disappeared back on the prairie all that time ago. And now she had fallen in love with the machinery and with the safety of this room. She was too scared to leave now, and she was dressing it up as personal choice.

'You'll have to come with us,' I said. 'The whole family has to be back together...'

Hannah shook her head sorrowfully at me. 'You can't tell her what to do, Lora. That's your problem. You go round telling everyone what to do. You think you know better than everyone.'

'But I had to!' I burst out, suddenly furious. 'I had to start making the decisions, didn't I? No one else was going to do it, after Da went. If I hadn't taken over ... we'd never have left the prairie! We would have ... would have...'

Hannah pulled a face. 'We would have what? Carried on living happily, as normal? Or would we have been *Disappeared*? You said yourself that wasn't such a bad thing. You said the Martian Ghosts were our friends, really. So would that have been so terrible?'

Her taunting words were making me think of Sook. It hadn't sunk in yet that I had seen her for the last time. Inside I was very shaken up. I was in no mood to argue with my little sister.

'I think they're coming for us,' said Peter, and, sure enough, the door swished open.

Only one of the Ancients had come to talk to us.

It was the smallest one, Arnold, with the kindly face and the twinkling black eyes. He had been kinder towards us than the others since we had been in the Underworld, and now they had chosen him as their spokesperson.

He was smiling, almost shyly. 'I've been delegated to bring you all before the Heart.'

'The Heart?'

Arnold bowed and said softly, 'All will be explained. You'll see, Lora. I hope you'll understand everything soon. Will you come with me?'

'Hold on,' I said. 'First I want to know where you're taking us, and why. For all we know you could be about to have us executed or something.'

He looked alarmed. 'Executed! Why … why, no! Why would we do such a thing? We couldn't bring ourselves to harm any of you.'

Something clenched in my gut at these words. 'What about the bodies we found in the cells? They'd wasted away to skeletons.'

He looked ashamed. 'You shouldn't have seen those rooms. They were our early guests in the labyrinth. Before we knew how to look after human beings properly. We made many mistakes at first…'

I was horrified.

'But we know better now. We would never harm any of you…'

I burst out: 'What about Watt, then? He came to harm, didn't he? You sure harmed him.'

Arnold looked worried, wringing his tiny fingers together. 'The Servo was in an area he shouldn't have been. You both were. My people hurried to the site of your transgression in order to prevent harm, not to cause it.'

This didn't make me feel any better.

Peter said, 'We don't trust you. We don't trust any of you. Lora's right. All these screens and stuff. The machinery. You've been trying to get us hooked on relying on this machine stuff. Lora's mum never wants to leave here because of it. And that's just how you like it, isn't it?'

The Ancient Arnold beamed calmly at Peter. 'Such an impulsive, shouty boy. Yes, you're quite right, of course. But we see everything the machinery brings as a pleasant reward for your attention and your devotion. It is our promise to keep you warm and fed and entertained and stimulated and safe ... *forever*. Now, what could be wrong with that?'

Toaster took us all by surprise then. His electronic voice tolled out like a bell. 'Because it is *false*! Because it is incarceration! You can't put human beings in cells like this and call it freedom and happiness. I know this much about human beings, after all my years of serving them: they thrive only when they are free.'

'Or perhaps,' chuckled the tiny Arnold. 'They thrive when they *believe* themselves to be free. That isn't the exact same thing, is it?'

'You are talking about illusions,' said Toaster. 'About living a life of illusions. That is no good, in the end.'

'Ah, my dear sunbed,' Arnold giggled. 'You speak as if from experience, don't you? Your own artificial mind has been dogged by illusions, has it not? And you have suffered delusions and brain-wipes and false memories and a return to factory settings? You've had quite a tricky time of it, haven't you? And what a long, long, incredibly long life you've had. Not bad for a simple window-cleaning Servo, eh?'

It was at that moment that Peter decided to show the old guy exactly how impulsive he was. 'Yeah, well, you didn't see this coming, did you?'

Ma gave a shriek as he lunged forward and seized hold of the Ancient One.

Arnold's body seemed so light and fragile in his hands that Peter might have broken every bone in his body.

That small room was filled with shouting and jostling figures for a few moments and even I was taken by surprise. I'd never have suddenly attacked Arnold like that, but Peter had had enough. He had the Ancient in a headlock and both of his stubby arms clutched in his fist.

'You're our hostage,' Peter said. 'You'll tell your friends we've got you hostage and we won't let you go unless they let us leave this place unharmed.'

The Ancient One coughed and winced, trying to speak. 'Peter, you're strangling him…' I said.

'Yeah, I'll throttle the life out of him if I have to.'

Ma was weeping, clutching Hannah to her. 'Lora, you can't let him do this. It's murder! It's a disgrace! They'll throw us all out! They've been so kind to us…'

Toaster said, 'I'm not sure if this is the wisest course of action…'

'Shut up!' Peter snapped at all of us. Even Karl started yapping worriedly. 'I mean it. I'll break this old guy's neck unless they let us out. Do you understand that? Will you tell your superiors?'

Arnold sighed. 'You understand so little about us. I have no superiors. We are all equal. And if you threaten one, you cannot harm the others. There are many more of us. My sacrifice will be of no importance to them.'

'I … I don't believe it,' Peter said. 'You're lying.' He looked wildly at the rest of us. 'He's bluffing, isn't he?'

'You can't threaten me,' said Arnold. 'I'm not scared of you.'

Peter shook him like a doll. 'But there's something you want from us, isn't there? There's something you people desperately want from us…'

'Oh yes,' said the Ancient. 'And if you'll set me down, I'll gladly tell you. I was going to tell you anyway. As I said earlier: I am going to take you to the Heart. *Our* heart.'

'Put him down, Peter,' I said. 'I think this means we're going to get some answers…'

17

We had no choice but to follow him.

Arnold looked relieved that Peter was no longer threatening to choke him. He even seemed pleased that we were consenting to come with him to look at this Heart.

Whatever that was.

'Ma?'

She shook her head dumbly. So did Hannah. 'We'd rather stay here. We'd rather watch the magic pictures.'

The Ancient coughed and looked at them gently. 'Madame Robinson, this concerns you and your daughter, also. What we Ancients are proposing is something that you must consider, too.'

Ma didn't look at all pleased about this. She became more nervous than ever. 'I thought you were happy for us to sit in our rooms, watching the screens?'

'Ah, yes, we are. We have learned so much from you that way. About your inner lives. So, so interesting. You human beings don't hold anything back, do you? So open. So transparent.'

The door opened and Arnold ushered us into the featureless corridor, wheezing gently. He was becoming a deeper shade of pinkish-blue, as if his confidence had started to return.

As we walked along behind, I sidled up to Peter. 'That was a good try.'

He pulled a face. 'I wouldn't really have killed him, you know.'

'I know that. But you scared him, whatever he said.'

'I don't know. They clearly don't think of themselves as individuals. They don't know fear in the way we do. That makes them powerful enemies.'

I turned to Toaster, to make sure that he was keeping notes on the route we were taking, deeper and deeper into the maze of corridors. We might need to break our own way out of here. Toaster was brilliant at schematics and creating maps. But even he looked perplexed by the twisting and turning of the smooth walls.

'Nothing is consistent here,' he frowned. 'The whole city is made of soft, malleable matter. Almost like alien flesh. I don't believe the tunnels stay in the same positions...'

I'd suspected as much. The subterranean city could reshape and disguise itself. It was completely possible that we'd never be able to find our way back out.

Arnold led us at a rapid pace, padding along on his flat feet. Now and then he'd look back at us with a gentle smile. How could I ever have thought he might feel sympathy for us? Or be even slightly on our side? It had been a pathetic hope.

Soon we became aware of a steady beating noise resounding through the corridors.

It was deeper than a noise you'd hear with only your ears. It reverberated through the walls and floor.

I could feel it deep in my chest. It was getting bigger and more profound with every step we took.

'Listen,' Peter said. 'Enough with the mysteries. What is this heart you were on about? Is it a place? A building? A treasure of some kind?'

The Ancient's face beamed brighter. 'It is and it isn't. It is all of us, and none of us living.'

'Riddles,' sighed Toaster. 'How dreary. My database has the solution to every known riddle mankind has created…'

'Riddles?' Arnold frowned. 'I don't seek to bamboozle you. I am telling you the truth. The Heart is the organ at the very centre of our Underworld. And it contains all of us who have passed on and moved to the next life.'

'What?' I gasped. 'The souls of all your dead?'

He shrugged. 'If that is how you like to express it, then yes. Soon I will join them, I believe. And then I will know much more about it.'

I didn't like the sound of any of this.

'There is no such thing as the soul,' stated Toaster flatly. 'Servos and humans both have a limited time to live, and then our bodies wear out finally and we are no more.'

'Ah,' chuckled the Ancient. 'And yet your soul moved from one machine to another, did it not, Toaster? You were tiny, and then you were great. And you have been repaired and refashioned so many times since then. And your soul has proved far more durable than your physical frame.'

Toaster looked annoyed by Arnold's logic.

'Besides,' added the Ancient. 'I and my kind are not remotely human.'

Now the pounding of that heartbeat noise was much louder and it filled our heads and dominated our thoughts.

A final door opened and we were gently ushered inside a very large room. It was a delicate orange-pink inside, and almost entirely empty.

'What is this?' Peter said. 'Another prison?'

There was something in the very centre of the room.

Something small.

As Arnold urged us forward I could see that the object was suspended in mid-air.

After a few steps it was plain to see what it was.

Karl started yapping as if he was hungry. Yes, there was a strange, meaty smell. There was a tang of fresh blood in the noisy air.

'You have got to be kidding,' Peter said. 'When he said "heart" I figured he was talking metaphorically, or something ... or it was a name for a sacred shrine or some dumb computer. Not this. Not ... an *actual heart*, just hanging there...'

It was larger than any heart I'd ever seen from beasts we had butchered at the Homestead. It was even bigger than the hearts we hewed out of the carcasses of burden beasts.

Muscle and fat. Chambers and veins and fleshy tubes.

This was a heart bigger than my head. It was bulbous and glistening in the soft light. Its noise kept on filling our heads.

'This is *us*,' the tiny Ancient creature said. 'This is all of us who have gone before. It is our collective will that has brought you people here. This is the moment we have brought you to.'

I did my very best to seem unimpressed. 'What does it want with us?'

Arnold smiled at me.

And so did all of his fellow Ancients, who were arriving in the orange chamber silently. All sizes and shapes, tall and spindly, squat and dumpy. Some of them smooth and glowing, others fuzzy with golden fur. Each of them was smiling ecstatically.

Of course they were happy. They had us exactly where they wanted us.

And at their head came the graceful form of Ma Taproot.

When we'd last seen her she had been lumbering and shambolic, but now she glided smoothly. Her tattered rags and wraps had been replaced by a beautiful golden robe that brushed the ground. Her whole demeanour was calm and poised. Light seemed to flood out of her face.

'Welcome to the Heart of Mars,' she said.

We stared at her as she sat on a throne beside the suspended heart. Arnold went to her and leaned against her knees. She stroked his head and toyed with his ears.

'This Heart contains the wisdom of all the Ancients,' Ma Taproot said. 'Everything we are is centred here.'

'We thought you were human,' Peter gasped out. 'When we met you in your tree…'

She smiled at him pityingly. 'Did you? Oh dear, no. I appeared to you looking a little more human simply to reassure you, and to put you at your ease. Similarly, the interior of my tree was created to make you feel at home. We didn't want to scare you or unnerve you, did we, everyone?'

The Ancients murmured softly. 'Oh no, not at all,' they chorused.

'The books on my shelves. Everything you saw. I suppose it was an illusion of sorts…'

'And this?' I asked.

'This is all real. Here you are at the centre of the labyrinth. Here you are at the heart of the story at last. Everything here is quite real.'

'What do you want from us?' I asked, staring back into Ma Taproot's face with all the bravery I could find.

'Your knowledge. Your knowledge is very special. We seek to add it to ours.'

I frowned. 'What knowledge do we have?'

'Star travel,' said Arnold, smiling as Ma Taproot fondled his ears. 'You humans have, buried somewhere deep inside you, the knowhow for getting to the stars. And we would like you to share that knowledge, please.' He chuckled at his own bland politeness.

I stared at Peter and at Toaster. It was just as Sook had said. Suddenly I felt like laughing. I turned back to Arnold, Ma Taproot and the others, and to that hideous, gory organ hanging in mid-air, and I told them, straight out: 'But we don't know *anything*. Don't you realise that?'

The Ancients shifted and stirred. They started muttering amongst themselves.

I laughed at them. 'We don't know anything about Starships or space travel or any of that stuff!'

Ma Taproot's patient smile faded slowly from her face.

I went on. 'How could we? All that knowledge was lost before I was even born…!'

'Liar!' someone called out.

Another of the Ancients joined in, 'You lie! You taunt us!'

Soon they were all screaming at me. 'You must know! You have to know! Tell us the truth!'

Their faces were twisted up. Their smiles had dropped. Finally, perhaps, they were showing their true feelings. They clenched their fists and shook them.

The Heart was pounding much louder now.

A little blood dripped from it to the floor.

Above the noise Arnold was shouting: 'Tell us! Tell us!'

His face had turned darker. He looked like the same friendly Arnold, but when he shouted he revealed those long, dagger-like teeth.

Ma Taproot rose to her feet and flung her hands into the air. She bellowed: '*Enough!*'

Suddenly we were standing in complete darkness.

It was like being shut in a small storeroom. I even heard the slam of a door.

But then I became aware that there were lights dancing around us. There were swathes of coloured lights, like scarves softly swaying. And at my feet ... I looked down and saw that my feet were standing on nothing at all.

I could see my friends, quite plainly, standing beside me. Peter, Toaster and Karl. They all looked shocked, too, to be suspended in the middle of nothing.

'I know what this is,' Toaster said softly. 'I have been here before.' There was a mournful note in his electronic voice.

'What is this place?' Peter asked him.

'It's the Ancients,' I realised. 'They're showing us something. Like with the machinery and the magic pictures. But this is more powerful...'

'It's an illusion, then, is it?' Peter was looking scared. He tried to move and found that he was floating, weightless in the dark. 'Is any of this real?'

Toaster's sensors chirruped and blinked. 'If this was real,

then you organic people would have suffocated by now. Look.' He waved one of his clamp-hands at the blackness about us. 'Do you see? We are in deepest space. That's what we are looking at now.'

We barely had time to digest this idea before the Starships came into view.

They were magnificent.

It was me who turned round and saw them first, and I gave out a squeaky cry. The others all whirled around. Our movements were slow and it was like swimming through molasses in a dream.

'The ten Starships from Earth,' Toaster said softly. There was awe in his voice. And pride, too, I decided, as if he was a part of this amazing spectacle. And I suppose he was. He had been aboard the *Melville*, hadn't he? Along with my family.

The Starships were immense and beautiful. Their smooth hulls soon filled up the vast dark skies around us and we found ourselves surrounded by the fleet.

They cut swathes through the darkness and the wreathing space mists. Asteroids and meteors clanked and bounced hopelessly off their sheer metal hides. The ships were silver and gold and bright scarlet. Their names were painted on their sides: *Hawthorne*, *Dickinson*, *Melville*. They seemed invincible, as they swam purposefully towards their destination.

We had seen the wreckage of these ships in the desert. We had visited the remains of the *Emily Dickinson*, and ventured into her shattered body. To see her resplendent and perfect like this was quite something.

'But how are we seeing this?' Peter gasped. 'Were these recordings made sixty years ago? But then, who was watching? Who was there to see?'

There came a delighted chuckling, rippling through the star-spattered darkness.

Then all at once Arnold was standing with us.

He slid his small hand into mine and squeezed gently. His face was screwed up with delight at our confusion.

'Why, naturally, *we* were here, Peter. The Ancients were here watching everything that transpired. Don't you see that yet? We've watched your people all this time.

'These Martian settlers in their beautiful ships, and also your own ancestors, too, two hundred years even before this, in your far less grand and elegant spacecraft.

'We watched you in your City. And we watched these people settle on the prairie. And well before that, we observed the civilisation you call the Martian Ghosts rise and fall in the dry, benighted lands of the west. We have seen it all unfold on Mars.'

Arnold smiled thoughtfully.

As his words sunk in we saw for the first time the world that the fleet of Starships was travelling to.

I held my breath and my head reeled.

For here was home.

Here was Mars.

Fiery crimson and gold. Flaring brilliantly in the blackness.

It signalled danger, surely? That scarlet orb didn't look welcoming or safe. And yet the ten Starships were streaking so confidently and gladly towards it.

What must they have been thinking as they headed this way? Were they excited? Were they fearful? Did they regret what they had left behind?

I wished that my grandma or Aunt Ruby were here right now, so that I could ask them…

Of course, Toaster was here.

'Do you remember, Toaster?' I asked.

'All of it,' he said. 'Every single second of it. They were terrified, naturally. But also triumphant. They thought they had beaten the odds. They were leaving behind a corrupt and polluted Earth. And they thought they were the first humans to get this far.

'And, of course, they were wrong. They had no inkling of the wonderful green glass City hiding inside its cunning centuries' old defences. And they were not to find out about it, were they, until quite recently, Lora? Until *we* made our journey across the wilderness.

'That was the first time, really, that the whole story came together.'

Peter and I stared at Toaster, seeing that he was quite right. Our part in this story of Mars was important.

We had been to secret places. We had found out things

no human had ever found out before. We had even penetrated the secrets of the Ancients.

Arnold was laughing again. He was distracted by the antics of Karl, who was chasing his tail in the weightlessness of space.

Then he looked at us sharply. 'Yes, you people are indeed important. You contain multitudes. You know everything. The secrets that we need for our own plans all lie within you. They lie within the very substance of your being.'

'We don't know any secrets,' I snapped.

'The knowledge of how these Starships were created, and how they operated, that is what we need from you. This stuff they called blue-crystal technology, and the meshing of the organic and the artificial. These are the things we need to know about, if we are to bring the Starships back to life.'

I was about to protest again that knowledge for humans doesn't work like that. Maybe it did for the Ancient Ones. They had a shared group-mind, so perhaps everything one knew was known by everyone else. Perhaps they were all one great big creature.

But humans weren't like that. My grandparents might have been the cleverest human beings to ever live (though I doubted that) but that meant nothing when it came to me. I had to learn my own stuff.

I was about to say this to him when I suddenly realised what he'd just said. 'Bring the Starships back to life?'

Arnold simply nodded, and waved at the retreating fins of the vast machines as they streaked ever closer to Mars. 'Of course. Didn't you suspect that was our aim? Their rotting skeletons lie beached in the sands only a matter of miles from our home.

'Their brains are still active. They are dormant but alive. We have long wanted to take them for ourselves and to rebuild and control them.

'We have dreamed of taking them and ourselves into the stars. We have much to offer the universe, you know.

'And you, Lora, and your friends, can help us do just that.'

And then, all at once – *wham*.

The darkness became brighter and brighter, searing our eyes.

Suddenly we were back in the chamber with that horrible heart and all the Ancients looking at us eagerly.

They were looking at us like they were waiting for us to say something. Ma Taproot had an urgent, crafty look on her face as she sat on her throne.

They wanted us to tell them we could help. To say that there was nothing we would rather do.

Before Peter or I could say anything, Toaster stepped grandly forward.

'We would be honoured to do anything we possibly can,' he said. 'To bring those Starships back to life for you.'

Then he bowed, deep and low, and all the Ancients were smiling again.

18

'Do you think they can do it?' Peter asked. 'Do you think they stand a chance of making the Starships work again?'

The Ancients had left us alone in a kind of antechamber for a while: to get our thoughts together, and to absorb everything we had learned. Arnold had brought us some strange-looking snacks and a flagon of delicious, foaming juice. I didn't care if there was poison or mind-controlling drugs or anything in it: I was thirsty and starving.

'I'm pretty confused now,' I admitted.

'But Toaster,' Peter was saying. 'Why would you promise them anything? Why would you tell them we'll help?'

Toaster was brusque. 'I'm in no mood to argue with some busker,' he snapped. 'Just tell him, would you, Lora?'

I was taken aback by the sunbed's rudeness.

'Toaster thinks it's an amazing idea to bring the Starships back to life. For all of us. We'd all benefit from that.'

Peter shook his head, clutching Karl to his chest. 'And they'd let us just stand by and watch, would they? They aren't doing this for anyone's benefit but their own, Lora. Can't you see what they are?'

Toaster frowned at him. 'They are the true, indigenous, original people of Mars,' he said. 'That's what we have learned today, isn't it? We were the ones who came blundering in, crash-landing on their beautiful world. We were the ones who terraformed and dabbled with its ecosystems. We have caused huge changes to Mars…'

'He's right, Peter,' I said. 'I'm surprised the Ancients didn't just wipe us out straight away. They must hate us…'

'No, they don't hate anyone,' said Toaster musingly. 'They are very wise and very old. They have great secrets and gifts they want to bestow upon the whole universe. That's what I sense from them. But they don't think about people in the way that we do. They think as a collective does: always for the greater good.'

Peter and I both gave Toaster a funny look, then looked at each other. He was going a bit mystical and cosmic in the way he was talking. I was sure we were both wondering if he was somehow being taken over.

'Their faith in us is clearly misplaced,' Toaster said. 'They made an understandable assumption that we would be as wise as your forebears: that humans retained knowledge in their DNA. Clearly that's how life works for the Ancients. I hope they won't regret that mistake. You shouldn't have admitted your ignorance. What if they decide they no longer need you?'

I gasped. Toaster was right. Perhaps their mistaken assumption was the only thing keeping us alive right now?

Then Peter said, 'We shouldn't talk too openly. I bet they're watching and listening in on us at this very moment.'

We stared at each other.

Then Peter whispered, 'When we were down inside the *Emily Dickinson*, we heard something, didn't we, Lora? Before the men from the prairie came riding up, and before your grandma started yelling?'

I thought back to those queer noises, coming from deep within the bowels of the ship. There had been a feeling, too. A glow of some sort. A kindling of warmth. Yes, it had felt like a presence, somehow. But there hadn't been time to think about it or explore further.

'You're right,' I said. 'We both felt it. There was life down there. Not living people or creatures or Servos. The ship *itself* was still alive somehow. And ... crying out.'

Toaster looked solemn. 'Yes, I have felt this too. For many years I have heard these distant voices. Even back when we lived on the Homestead. I thought I was malfunctioning. I thought they were memory circuits fizzing in my head. I told no one, in case your father had me deactivated. Who would want a Servo who thought he could hear voices calling out to him?'

'So you've always known the Starships were still alive, even if you didn't realise it?'

'Alive and in pain. I see that now. Calling out to us. Wanting to be rescued.'

'Then if they're alive we ought to cooperate with the Ancients,' said Peter. 'And help them.'

'What I don't understand is why all ten ships crashed in the first place,' I said. 'Why all ten? And why all at the same time? Weren't they any good at landing?'

'Surely you know?' Toaster looked surprised. 'Surely your Grandma and Ruby must have told you?'

I shook my head. 'That bit of the story they never discussed. Don't you remember, Toaster? They never told anyone about the last day on board the *Melville*, or the other ships. It was something they didn't like talking about.'

'Perhaps it is for the best that they never told you what went on, that last day aboard the *Melville*,' said Toaster darkly.

We were interrupted by Arnold.

'Are you refreshed?' He seemed sprightly and enthusiastic. 'Perhaps we had better begin.'

I nodded. 'And what do we have to do?'

'You're going to travel to the site of the crash-landing all those years ago. The Valley of the Starships. And you're going to bring them back to life.'

'Er … OK,' I said.

'I believe you are resourceful,' the old creature said. 'We believe you have many gifts at your disposal. Surprising gifts. Magical gifts. You will do as we command you, we are quite confident of that.'

'You are?' asked Peter. 'And why's that?'

'You will do as we tell you because you will remember that we still have Lora's mother and her sister in their luxurious cells, deep within our labyrinth.'

I gasped at this. Arnold's tone hadn't altered in the slightest. His expression was still mild and benign. And yet this was clearly a threat.

He went on: 'They are contented and warm, and watching their magic pictures, thinking they are safe, but it would take only the slightest effort from us to snuff out their lives. A hypnotic suggestion, encoded in the pictures we show them, encouraging them to stop breathing. There are all kinds of possibilities, but please be assured: they are at our mercy. And so, you will do exactly what we want. You will bring those Starships back to life.'

Perhaps there had been something strange in the food and drink we hadn't been able to resist, because, from that moment on, something peculiar happened to my perceptions of the time and space around us. Everything seemed to stretch and distort...

I was expecting a long, arduous journey back up through the waxy corridors of the labyrinth, back up into the wooded world of Ma Taproot, deep beneath the swamplands. It would take us days to make our way back through those difficult places. And who knew what kind of enemies or creatures we might encounter en route?

I thought about all the people we had left behind on various stages of our travels. Were my grandma and Uncle Thomas and all their robots still at Ma Taproot's tree? Or had they returned to their camp in the swamp as the magic pictures had shown me? And what about Ruby and her men in their wooden town? Had they found our abandoned burden beasts and figured that we had perished in the desert?

And what about Da, alone in the City Inside? I was depending on Al to go and help him…

We were all so split up and separate. And now we were being forced to leave Ma and Hannah behind again.

I was starting to feel that we had made a rotten failure of our mission. What had we accomplished? Sure, we had learned a lot. But what use was it all?

That wouldn't bring back poor little Watt, would it?

Or Sook.

It was no use having these mawkish thoughts. It was no use being self-pitying. I had to keep myself together. As ever, people were depending on me.

The journey back up to the surface was nothing like I imagined it was going to be.

Arnold spread his arms wide and issued a series of commands at the machine in our cell. A single magic picture opened up like a giant eye before us.

'This, my friends, is a special picture. Even more powerful and fantastic than those you have already encountered.'

'Oh yes?' I was in a sceptical mood. This little creature

was so softly spoken, and yet he was holding us all to ransom. He had all the power and could make us do anything he wanted. I felt like pushing him over and kicking him at that moment. I could have set Toaster on him, or Peter again. But I didn't dare.

'The desert looks so real…' said Peter, suddenly, stepping forward.

It was a stunningly realistic picture, it had to be said. The sands were jewelled and the skies arching above the rocky valley were a delicate pink with orange overtones.

It was early morning on the surface of Mars. A warm wind blew through the valley, lifting veils of glittering sand and depositing them in new formations.

It was mesmerising.

Something within me was hankering to be there. I realised I was missing the warmth and the softness of the surface of my world.

'Step through,' Arnold chuckled. 'I told you it was a special picture. You may simply step through.'

'You've got to be kidding me…' I said, staring intently at the edges of the screen.

Peter and Karl were already walking up to the frame and stepping through.

'Lora, it's warm! It's so beautiful … feeling the breeze on your face again. It's … breath-taking!' He was laughing and Karl was bouncing about on the shifting sands, yapping at him.

I blinked. They were actually in the picture.

Beside me Toaster was surging forward, muttering to himself. 'A transmutational beam … of course! Theoretically, of course … it's possible … but I have never seen…'

And before I could stop him or warn him, he too had stepped into the picture and the Ancient at my side hooted with laughter.

'Why so shy? Why so scared? Come on, Lora! You must step through! It's the new way to travel. Isn't it a miracle? I thought you relished new experiences! I thought you liked to be the first and the most courageous! Be strong! Be brave!'

Now Arnold was tugging at my hand. His tiny fingers squeezed mine together.

I stepped into the picture.

And then we were all together.

We were standing outside under the blazing sun and it felt so wonderful. How long had we been underground?

All that artificial light and air. There had never been a whisper of a breeze. It was like being dead, being down in that perfumed labyrinth. But out here we were back in the roasting brilliance.

'But … but where are we?' I turned to ask the Ancient, who looked strangely pale and vulnerable in the open air. 'This valley… We could be anywhere…'

'Anywhere,' cackled the Ancient. He started dancing about on the sand, dashing around our small party and laughing at our puzzled expressions. 'Anywhere and anywhen! *Anywhen*, eh! What about that?'

I had no idea what he was talking about. But right then there was a noise that took all our minds off the nonsense he was spouting.

'Look!' cried Toaster, his voice booming out above the screaming, shrieking noise.

Suddenly much louder, the noise echoed through the valley and it was almost too much for human ears to take.

My eardrums went scratchy and painful and sound cut out completely for a few moments.

I saw Peter whirling about, staring into the sky and shielding his eyes. I saw Toaster standing impassively, craning his telescopic neck and boggling at the shapes emerging from the scarlet depths of the sky.

I stared and stared and my mind refused to comprehend what it was I was looking at.

Like ten vast skyscrapers they came hurtling through the immense bowl of the sky. They were the ten gleaming Starships from Earth.

Somehow we were here, witnessing their arrival on Mars.

The tiny Ancient had his hands in the air again, weaving strange, arcane patterns with his gnarled fingers. It was as if he was conducting their noisy music, and communing with the ships as they sailed and soared above us… He smiled happily to himself.

All of this happened so very quickly. He clicked his fingers. The ships were falling, one at a time, out of the perfect sky.

We were here at the crash-landing. We were actually witnessing planet-fall. Somehow we were seeing the very start of the story.

Toaster seized hold of me. 'We have to run…!' he howled, right in my ear.

Then in all the noise and the confusion that followed, I blacked out.

19

I woke from confused dreams on the burning sand.

The noise was gone. There was silence and the moaning of wind against jagged rock.

How had we observed those ships in flight? How had we been able to see them crash land, so long ago?

Now it was all over, and we were back in our time.

The others were awake, dishevelled, and waiting for me. Arnold was giving me a strange smile.

I joined them and we stared at the Valley of the Starships.

In the heat haze of midday the wreckage was still there, most of it buried under the dust: all ten Starships of the famous Earth fleet. We stared for several long moments, holding our breath under the searing sun.

Tail fins sprouted from the jewel-like sand. The vast bellies and shattered hulls were immense, almost unfathomable. From this vantage point we could count evidence of all ten ships.

'It's a graveyard,' Peter said. 'It feels almost wrong our being here, doesn't it?'

I thought about the Adamses, back in Our Town. They would come out to this place several times each year, wouldn't they? They specialised in plundering the Starships and selling anything they found to the descendents of the travellers.

Strange to think of that now: a detail from another life.

Back then, when I was a little kid, all I knew were the confused tales Grandma would tell us, and the fancy goods brought back to the Adams' Emporium: shrimps and sweets and soaps.

Arnold held up both hands as if he was having some kind of mystical experience, perhaps praying.

'Behold!' he cried out, and giggled. 'Don't they make you proud? It was you people who built these marvellous machines. You had the ingenuity and the wherewithal. You crossed the barren nothingness between your home and ours. Can you imagine it now? Can you even believe that it was true?'

'The human race is remarkable,' said Toaster. 'It has achieved much.'

The small Ancient smiled at this, baring his surprising fangs again.

'Oh, Toaster. You're a supreme human achievement yourself, aren't you? Do you realise that? Just how special you are?'

'Yes,' said the sunbed huffily. 'As a matter of fact, I do.' And then he started stumping off down the dune, towards the closest of the ships. Karl the cat-dog set off happily after him, joyously skipping on the soft sand.

'Toaster seems to know where he's heading,' Peter shrugged.

'Yes, he does, doesn't he?' said the Ancient musingly. 'We would do well to listen to the Servo's instincts, and to follow him now...'

'What do you mean?' I asked suspiciously. Arnold was up to something I realised. He knew much more than he was letting on.

'Blue-crystal technology,' Arnold said, and started leading the way down the dune. Up here, in the bright light of day, he was less nimble than he'd been in his own, underground world. 'Have you heard of it?'

'Kind of,' I said. 'It's something very advanced, isn't it? From Earth?'

'It was cutting edge on Earth,' Arnold said. 'The most up-to-the-minute science. We don't understand it ourselves. It's not *our* kind of thing at all. We hardly understand our own technology, to tell you the truth.' He laughed shrilly again. I was starting to wonder about his sanity. 'But those ships had it in them. That's what they had. The stuff of dreams. They sailed like a whisper. They zoomed and caromed at the speed of thought. They crossed distances more easily than had ever been possible before. And your Toaster – he's got the same stuff inside him. Blue crystal. It's what makes him so ... different. So special.'

Peter looked thoughtful. 'He *is* special, isn't he? He's not like any other Servo-Furnishing I've ever met. I mean, he's clever, of course. And you believe that he really does care for his charges and everyone in his care, and he's been through so much.'

'But there's something more,' I nodded. We were walking down the steep sides of the dune now, into the valley proper. The thick red sand was slithering dryly and drawing us down towards the Starships, like some heavy drag of gravity was working on us.

'There's always been something more, something extra about Toaster. We always took it for granted, because he was the only Servo we knew.'

Peter was watching the sunbed as he marched ahead unerringly towards the tall, ribcage structure of the nearest vessel. 'It's as if he's alive,' he said suddenly. 'That's the difference with Toaster. He's a living being.' He looked at Arnold. 'That's what it is, isn't it? That's what you mean?'

Arnold twinkled away, and shrugged his sloping shoulders. 'I wonder if that's what I mean. Possibly. But Toaster has got the blue crystals, just as the ships had. Bio-mech. It was the very latest thing.'

Ahead Toaster waved both telescopic arms at us and turned up his volume. 'This ship! This is the least damaged overall, I believe. This is the least spoiled, and the least scavenged.'

'Toaster is very important,' the Ancient. 'To all of us. In fact, you might say that he is central to all our concerns. Yes…'

Toaster shouted to us: 'It's the *Kurt Vonnegut*. And I detect … signs of life!'

We hurried over there, wading through the slippery and shifting sands, our minds buzzing with questions.

'Life?' I gasped, as we came level with the sunbed. 'How can there be life? What do you mean … people? Survivors?'

Toaster frowned at me. 'No, not people. Of course not people. All the people that survived explored and found the prairies, as you know. No one stayed here in the Valley of the Starships. They left our past lives behind.'

'Then what? Who?'

Arnold clapped his hands with glee. He waggled his stumpy fingers in the direction of the rupture in the silver skin of the ship.

'Shall we investigate for ourselves? Shall we see? Oh, I love this bit. I love being up here in the actual world above. How very real it all is!'

Peter muttered to me as we all made our way towards the hole in the side of the ship. 'I don't like this, and I don't trust that little guy in the slightest.'

'I know,' I said. 'But Toaster won't let anything bad happen. If need be, I'm sure he could overpower Arnold…'

'I don't think it's that easy,' Peter said. 'I think Arnold's powerful. All this chuckling and stuff, it's to put us off guard. I feel like all the power of the Ancients and that strange heart of theirs and Ma Taproot herself … I feel like it's all with us, every step we take up here on land … it's all bound up in that tiny little body of Arnold. They've got us doing exactly what they want…'

I said, 'And what they want is aboard the Starships?'

'We're going along with their plans. We're helping them. And I don't think we're gonna like what they want to do…'

The *Kurt Vonnegut* was like nowhere we had ever been before.

Whereas the *Emily Dickinson* had been a hollow shell, all upside down with dark hollows echoing fathoms deep, this ship was more like it would have been in its glory days. Somehow it had touched down and done very little damage to itself. The main hatchway was even working okay. With a little leverage Toaster had it open, and a set of carpeted stairs extended to meet us.

'Funny that this ship is the most perfectly preserved,' the sunbed commented. 'It wasn't the most opulent or even the most robust. The *Melville*, which the Robinsons and Ruby and her father were aboard – that one was the envy of the fleet. The *Vonnegut* was the smallest. Slightly battered, compared with the others. It had logged more hours in space. Yet somehow here it is, looking almost like it did on the day we left Earth. Curious.'

It was dark aboard, naturally, and Toaster turned his tanning lamps on as bright as he could, creating a broad, hot beam that cast alarming, jagged shadows.

Room after room opened up before us. Toaster explained we were in the chambers that the passengers would never have seen. These were the crew rooms and the service areas. They were drab and functional. But, amazingly, they had floors and walls and nothing had been ruptured or twisted out of shape. The whole ship was lying at a slight angle, which meant we were walking up hill the whole time, which became harder and more slippery the deeper we went.

'I have the schematics in my memory banks, of course,' Toaster told us. 'I have the plans of all ten ships, buried deep in my brain. I never thought I'd need them again, so it's taking me a little while to process the images. But I believe this is the right way to the bridge.'

'These signs of life, Toaster,' Peter asked. 'Are they any clearer? What do you feel now?'

The sunbed frowned. 'Feel? I'm not sure I feel anything at all, Peter. But I am hearing something, I believe. Something long-buried, long-dormant. Something that feels like it's perhaps time to wake up.'

Toaster paused and shone his bright beam up the walls and along the ceiling of the long corridor we were climbing. His words echoed strangely up the sloping depths.

'This is wonderful,' said the Ancient. 'We have been here, of course. My people have probed these delicate vessels with our minds and the mind of our marvellous machinery, but we couldn't hear like Toaster can. We were aware of something … *interesting*. But we aren't gifted like you are, Toaster.'

Toaster didn't say anything to Arnold. He merely set off again, striding into the unknown.

Peter glanced at me. 'Those two seem to have their own separate agendas.'

'Toaster won't let us down,' I said.

'Karl, come here. I don't want you wandering off, and getting lost inside this thing…'

The metal corridors wound and twisted as much as the labyrinth of the Ancients. We caught glimpses of the lounges and recreation areas and restaurants where the Earth people would have gathered and relaxed and whiled away their days during their journey from Earth. The *Vonnegut* might have been the least luxurious of the Starships, but it still seemed pretty stylish to me. Everything was purple and orange, with fuzzy fabrics and amazing painted murals everywhere.

'It's the solar system,' Peter said, as we stood before one painting, which filled one vast wall. 'You know, like the planets in the planetarium, back in the City Inside.'

We stared at the arrangement of heavenly bodies, each painted in livid shades of green, orange or blue. Here was our diminutive planet, Mars, strung out along the massive distance between beads.

And there was the vast cool orb of the Earth. Try as I might, I couldn't summon up any feeling for that blue world. It wasn't mine. The picture was completely abstract to me. I just couldn't imagine being on another planet or how travel between them was even possible.

At last, just when our legs were aching from the upward incline, and it seemed that the *Vonnegut* would never end, we came to the bridge.

It was spectacular.

I was expecting something at least as grand as the green glass control room of the Sky Saucer built by Professor Swiftnick, but this went way beyond. The bridge was a room at least as big as a luxury apartment and it had one glass wall that must once have looked onto the vastness of space. Now, of course, all it looked at was the dark, impacted sand it had burrowed into when it crashed.

Peter was leaning over the control panels. There were loads of them, all covered with buttons and switches and metal wheels. Everything looked hideously complicated.

'Don't touch anything!' I warned him.

'I don't suppose anything I touched would make much difference,' he smiled. 'It's all switched off.'

Arnold was hoisting himself into a padded command chair. It looked awkward, his limbs being rather short, and the chair tilted at a strange angle. He huffed and puffed as if getting comfortable was taking up all of his attention.

Toaster, meanwhile, was shuffling from panel to panel of instruments, looking rapt and awestruck. He looked like someone in a kind of sacred, holy place. I guess that's exactly what it was to him.

'Could you have worked all this stuff, Toaster?' I touched his arm and disturbed the spell he was in.

'At a pinch, I could have,' he said, very solemnly. 'But it was never my role. And neither was it any one person's sole responsibility. The Starships were automated. They pretty much ran themselves, you know. They were fantastic creations. Humankind had really outdone themselves.'

'Oh yes!' said Arnold keenly. He moved towards the instrument panel before him and laid his cheek against the coloured glass. His face crumpled as he smiled, touching all the switches, one at a time. 'Oh, it's perfect. It's state-of-the-art. It's a piece of enchantment.'

Peter pulled a face. 'It looks pretty unreliable to me. A few old wires. Some clunky controls. Are you saying that people actually entrusted their lives to … *this*?'

'Oh yes,' said Toaster. 'It might look like disused machinery, but just think of what it could do. You really shouldn't judge by appearances, Peter.'

Peter flushed. 'I try not to.'

'Well, good,' said Toaster. 'Look at our friend here. He's the most inconsequential-looking creature you've ever met, isn't he? He looks like a miniature burden beast from the desert, walking on his two hind legs. And yet we know him to be part of the most Ancient and powerful race your kind have ever encountered. In fact, hardly any human beings have ever communicated with a sentience as advanced as his.'

Arnold giggled and gave Toaster a friendly tap. 'Oh, you.' Then his soft face suddenly went sly. 'Though you are, of course, quite right.'

I had to ask a question that was nagging at me. 'So why have you led him here, Toaster? If he and his people are so powerful, why have you led them straight to the controls of this Starship?'

'They can't do anything with it,' said Peter. 'It's dormant. It won't ever fly again. It can't be brought back to life, can it.' He stared at the rest of us. 'Can it?'

'I want to see these ships live again,' said Toaster simply. 'If I have life, then so should they. If there's the slightest chance for them…'

There was a shrill bleeping noise, coming from somewhere.

There. On the panel. Where Arnold had laid his ancient head for just a moment, as he hugged the console.

One single light was flashing.

Aquamarine. Urgent.

'*Alive* … after all this time,' said Toaster, with rising excitement in his voice.

20

The Ancient was looking at me with a strange sadness in his black eyes. 'We thought you were the ones who would help us. We were wrong, weren't we?'

'What do you mean?'

He sighed. 'We thought you humans had the knowledge in your flesh and bones, in the watery cells that make up your alien bodies. In the soggy matter of your human brains. We thought you had passed on the knowledge of space travel, one generation to the next, in that way...'

'You over-estimated us,' said Peter. 'We don't know anything. Hardly anything at all...'

'So you kept us imprisoned, brought us here ... and all of this was because you thought we could help you travel into space?' I was still amazed they could have got it so wrong. 'None of that was passed on to us. These ships are just wrecks to us.'

That blue light was still flashing on the desk. But then there was another, and then another. Others were joining it. The whole room was lighting up.

'Okay, so the ship's alive...' Peter said. 'And that's

amazing, of course. A living ship! After all this time! But what does it mean? We can't do anything with it. We can't take it anywhere … can we?' He gazed around in awe at the very idea.

Arnold pounded his skull with both fists. 'Oh, we have been foolish to put our faith in you people. And we thought we would do great things for all our races. We thought we could unite us all … Martians and ghosts, hybrids and humans … Ancients and all … we thought we could all travel to the stars together!' His eyes were blazing ferociously.

I felt like laughing at the audaciousness of his plan.

'But who wants to go into space? Grandma said it was dark and dreary and freezing. They were glad to come to Mars. They were even glad to crash land and never have to be in space again.'

Arnold shook his head. 'Just think of what is out there. The worlds and stars. The treasure. Knowledge. Things we don't even know about. Things we would struggle to comprehend. Don't you want that?'

'I…' I stared at him. 'I don't know.' More lights were coming on. There was no ignoring the surge of humming power that was filling the room and causing the metal floor beneath our feet to tremble. 'No! I don't! I don't want space and … unknown treasures. Do you know what that sounds like to me?' I was having to shout now, as the machinery around us grew louder. 'It sounds like more mysteries! And do you know what? I am just sick of mysteries! I've had enough of mysteries and adventures for one whole lifetime! Why me, eh? Why is it always me?'

The Ancient was staring at me, and now there was amusement in his dark eyes. He giggled at me. 'Hoo hoo hoo!'

'I don't want to explore,' I shouted. 'You can stick your rotten space and all the other stars and planets where the sun don't shine. Do you know what I'd settle for? A bit of peace and safety here on Mars. I'd settle for my family being safe, and all together, and happy, for once. I'd settle for some normality, thank you very much.'

'Are you finished?' asked Arnold.

I nodded. I felt a lot better for ranting.

'Good. You see, I have lost faith in your humankind and the knowledge you might or might not have access to. I see now that you had, all along, the means of storing everything you ever knew. You failed to remember things because you had already invented faithful receptors. You relied on them to remember for you, and yet you treated them so badly. So shockingly. You treated them like servants.'

Peter gasped. 'The Servo-Furnishings. That's who you mean, isn't it?'

'You've bequeathed everything you know to them. And to Toaster in particular. Toaster is the most valuable of them all.'

We all looked at Toaster.

But, for once, Toaster wasn't listening.

He was busily at work on the control console. His clamp-like hands were dancing across the toggles and switches. His glass face was bathed with iridescent light and that pounding noise from deep within the *Vonnegut* was resounding through his whole metal shell. It was as if Toaster was vibrating with the energy of the ship itself.

'Toaster!' I yelled over the confusing noise and light. 'What are you doing?'

'I … I don't even know!' he shouted back, echoing what I'd just said. I saw then that he couldn't stop his hands working the controls. It was as if the inner workings of the Starship had somehow reached out, tempted him, and grabbed hold of him. And now it wouldn't let go.

'Hoo hoo hoo!' shrilled Arnold, clutching his knees with excitement. 'This is it! It's happening now! It's really going to happen!'

The floor lurched and buckled beneath our feet. What had felt solid was rippling and bouncing and throwing us into the air. Karl was barking wildly and jumping up at Peter, but his owner couldn't give him any reassurance. 'What's happening, Lora?'

Something was happening to the dingy screen.

The darkness of the sand we were buried in was shifting and blurring. It was moving and tumbling round in a kaleidoscopic haze.

'I think we might be sinking!' I yelled out, horrified. 'I think we might be sinking even deeper into the valley!'

'If that happens, we've had it. The hatchway was open… The sand will flood in… If we don't get crushed, we'll suffocate slowly…'

Still Toaster's hands were busy with the controls. Both he and the console were pulsating with coloured light. I made to touch him, but a fierce crackle sent me reeling backwards.

The whole Starship juddered violently once more. We were moving … and the screen was crackling chaotically.

'Don't touch him, Lora,' Arnold shouted. 'Toaster is at one with the Starship *Vonnegut* now! Its dormant blue-crystal energy belongs to him! And his knowledge is flowing into its heart! It's working! It's all working better than we could have imagined!'

Peter grabbed hold of Arnold angrily a second time. I thought he was going to punch him or shake his tiny form to pieces.

'But we're sinking into the sands! We'll all be killed! What use is that?'

The Ancient laughed in his face. 'Don't you see? Can't you see? Everything is actually going to turn out perfectly…!'

The noise reached a crescendo then and the Starship gave a violent spasm that knocked us all off our feet.

By the time we clambered up off the floor we were in flight.

I had a thumping head and was relieved that the whole ship had stopped rocking and bouncing about.

Instead we were hovering smoothly on the air, high above the Valley of the Starships.

I stood slowly on wobbly legs, like a newborn burden beast. The view from the screen was like one from the tallest mountains of Mars, or like a glimpse of the world I got when I was flying with Sook. The panorama beyond the valley was vast and beautiful.

'I can't believe it either,' Peter said, still supporting me. 'He got this old bucket floating again. We're just hanging above the valley. It's like magic.'

It didn't feel like we were aboard an old bucket now. The Starship was humming and throbbing with energy. It was alive all around us; I could feel it.

Toaster was no longer standing with his hands on the controls. He was backing away, slowly. He was staring at Arnold.

The Ancient was in command of the Starship *Vonnegut* now.

He was holding something in his tiny hands.

I blinked and rubbed my eyes. I couldn't believe what I was looking at.

Beside me I heard Peter give a strangled gasp of disgust.

Arnold was holding the Heart of Mars.

It had materialised in his hands and was dripping dark blood on to the control console. And, as we watched, the ancient organ was pulsating with bright, living colour.

'How did he do that?' Peter asked. 'How did he bring it here?'

'It is what is called a gestalt creature, which means it is composed of many living parts that are linked together,' said Toaster. 'That is, it's all one being. The outer aspects we have seen – Arnold, the other Ancients, Ma Taproot, and the Heart itself – they are all part of the same organism. They are all, collectively, the Heart of Mars. And now it is in control of this living Starship.'

Buttons and lights were blinking of their own accord. Arnold looked as if he were directing everything with the sheer force of his will.

'What have you done, Toaster?' Peter shouted. 'You brought the ship back to life and you've handed it over to him!'

'I couldn't stop it,' Toaster muttered. 'I … I feel most strange. It was difficult, disengaging myself from the mind of the ship. It was reaching out and trying to absorb me. I only just managed to break away…'

'Toaster, come here,' said Arnold. 'We need your help.'

'No,' I said to the sunbed. 'Don't be part of this, Toaster. Don't help them any more…'

'Lora, I…' he stammered. 'I … I must…'

Arnold said, 'Just you wait and see how wonderful this will be. When I reach out with my mind, and wake up the other nine Starships … one at a time. Do you believe me when I tell you that I'm calling out now, deep underground, calling out to their slumbering souls?'

The gory, glowing heart in his hand changed colours from burning orange to the deepest, most beautiful blue.

'You can wake them all up?' I asked. 'Not just this one?'

Arnold sighed happily. 'I can feel all their dormant minds, waking up now, filled with questions. And they are all so pleased, so excited, at the thought of flying again. Of returning to the stars…'

'He's talking about them as if they truly are living beings,' Peter said. 'Is that what the blue-crystal technology really is? A way of bringing inanimate matter to … life?'

Toaster nodded. 'Arnold is telling the truth. I think it's all quite real. I can feel those presences under the sand. I can sense their questing minds. They're … they're calling out to me, Lora!'

I knew what we had to do. 'We have to get him away from here, Peter. Away from Arnold and this bridge…'

Peter nodded.

Then suddenly Arnold was calling out. 'There's a new arrival in the valley.'

'What?' I asked. 'Who?' I hoped it was something or someone who could help us.

21

'This ship was equipped with lasers,' Toaster told us calmly. 'But they weren't really intended for fighting. They were actually for disintegrating asteroids and other bits of space junk that the *Vonnegut* might have encountered on its journey to Mars.'

'Lasers! Oh, look!' cried Arnold, tapping his stubby fingers against the relevant controls. 'Oh, er ... oh dear. I seem to have ... um, activated them...'

He seemed to have no idea of the danger he had just unleashed. Nor did he seem concerned about halting those deadly lasers.

'Stop this at once!' said Toaster. 'You can't bring this vessel's weapons back online!'

'I appear to have done so ... oh dear!'

I clutched Peter's shoulder. 'We've got to get away and warn whoever it is arriving in the valley.' Then I did what Grandma would have done, and started yelling at Toaster. 'Come on, Toaster. Let's find a way off this thing.'

'I'm not sure I can,' said the sunbed shakily. 'I can feel this vessel wanting to fuse itself with my body and mind. And I can't just leave the Ancients in control of this vessel.

I must stay here … and do what I can to help Arnold …
I must learn to control these weapons. They may be
malfunctioning after so long in the desert sand, and he
doesn't appear to understand their lethal power… My duty
is to protect you all.'

Peter shouted, 'We all get to make up our own minds.
We all create our own destinies! Even Servos can!'

Toaster shook his head sorrowfully. 'No. I have a duty.
To serve the Robinsons. To protect human life. I must do
my very best at all times. And I must stay here and prevent
the Ancients from causing harm.'

There was a new and horrible noise as even more of the
lasers screeched and whined. Bolts of blue fire were
cascading from the nose of the *Vonnegut* and ricocheting
wildly around the valley. We could see them on the screen
as they liquefied rock and turned the sand into glass.

'N-no!' Toaster cried out. 'S-stop this! Stop firing!'

The lasers stuttered and paused as Toaster wrestled
mentally with the inner workings of the ship.

The noise was intense and the *Vonnegut* shuddered all
around us. The sunbed screamed as the lasers blazed into
life again.

The Ancient howled. 'Oh, the Earth people knew all
about creating weapons, didn't they?'

Toaster suddenly shouted out: 'Deck Five, Lora. Escape
pod F. It's still active. You can get down there … tell the
Authorities what is h-happening…'

'No! Don't go!' shrieked Arnold, seeing that we could slip out of his grasp.

'But Toaster … you have to come with us,' I yelled.

'I can't…' he gasped, clearly speaking with great difficulty.

Peter was already hustling me and Karl away from the control room. 'Quickly, before Arnold thinks of a way to keep us here.'

He was right. We had to go, but my every instinct warned against leaving Toaster. I channelled my grandma and her most hectoring, bullying tone.

'Toaster, you are coming with us. Right now! I refuse to let you stay here. Grandma and the others would never forgive me. You're coming with us!'

Then, with a wrenching cry, Toaster seized control of his limbs and moved away from the control console.

'Just leave him to it!' I yelled. 'As a member of the Robinson family, I *command* you, Toaster!'

It seemed that family loyalty meant more to Toaster than anything.

He started to run after us, out of the control room. His footsteps clanged heavily against the metal floor.

Then we were running down corridors after Peter and Karl.

'Noooo!' howled the Ancient behind us. He was hooked to the consoles and the Heart. There was nothing he could do.

And so we ran.

I was glad of Peter's sense of direction, as he counted the turnings we raced around, and staircases we thundered down.

As we made our way to Deck Five and the escape pod, the *Vonnegut* continued to lurch and buck through the air. The walls shuddered and groaned in protest.

We could still hear, even this deep inside the ship, the screeching of the lasers firing wildly about the valley.

'They're malfunctioning! Did you notice?' Peter asked, as we paused for breath, steadying ourselves against the bulkhead. 'They were firing off in every direction.'

Toaster slowed to a halt beside us. 'Their workings have corroded over the past six decades under the sand. It's lucky the whole thing hasn't simply exploded, taking all of us with it.'

'That's good,' said Peter. 'It means that evil old imp can't aim them properly.'

We both knew that he could still destroy the mysterious approaching vehicle by accident: huge volleys of random laser bolts could be just as effective as well-placed ones.

'And what about the other Starships in the valley?' gasped Peter. 'They're alive! What if they get shot to pieces?'

'We've got to hope Ma Taproot can stop this madness…' I said.

Toaster looked worried and ashamed. 'I should have

stayed on the bridge. Why did you command me to run away?'

'Because you're our sunbed,' I told him. 'And we love you.'

Peter said, 'That's all very touching, but what we have to think about right now is getting ourselves to safety.' He looked thoughtful, puzzling something out, and then he let out a cry. 'Here, this is it.'

There was a small door in the corridor.

'Through here?'

He nodded. 'It might be a bumpy landing…'

I clambered into a cushioned room.

It was quite a squeeze for Toaster, but he managed.

Peter closed the door behind us. Soft lights came on.

He was examining a simple control panel. 'Seems easy enough…' There was a large red button. It was obviously the one to press.

'Karl, come here…' I urged the cat-dog on to my knee. He was shivering and alarmed.

Peter slammed his palm against the button…

'Hello there!' trilled a voice we'd never heard before. 'I am your friendly and oh-so-efficient rescue pod!'

Karl started yapping fiercely at once, and strained to jump up at the hidden speakers.

'What is this?' Peter asked worriedly.

'Don't mind me!' carolled the voice. 'I am your fully

automated rescue pod and, since you have climbed aboard and triggered the vital red button, I imagine something drastic and rather horrible has happened upon the *Vonnegut*, huh? Well, never mind, and please strap in carefully as we prepare to eject with alacrity! Your precious human lives are safe with SKP; though, of course, you must not take this as any kind of legally binding guarantee of survival or freedom from horrible mishap. Disengaging … now!!'

Peter looked confused as we all struggled with straps and clasps and the escape pod started screeching and groaning around us. Clearly, after years of neglect in the desert the workings had corroded, and SKP was having trouble freeing itself from the belly of the vast ship.

'Oh, SKP! I get it,' I shouted over all the noise. 'Escapee, do you see?'

Toaster rolled his eyes. 'They insisted on giving simply everything a personality, back in those days.'

Peter yelled: 'We're gonna be smashed to bits, aren't we?'

'Never fear!' came the sugary voice of SKP. 'This pod is cushioned and protected against forty-eight per cent of feasible space accidents. Though it seems that sixty years have somehow passed without my noticing and … erm … my circuitry has decayed rather more than I'd like and … oh dear. Never mind! Don't worry, human beings and small, dog-like creature with metal legs! Everything is going to be absolutely fine…!'

With that the voice of SKP was drowned out by the clatter and howling of its own engines and the almighty splintering noise that came from it wrenching away from the hull of the *Vonnegut*.

We were thrown about and turned head over heels, screaming and shouting inside the cushioned confines. All the lights went out, and I was sure I heard the robot voice swearing and cursing in the dark.

Luckily, we didn't have very far to fall. This wasn't an average accident in space or in orbit that SKP had clearly been designed for. We were only a few hundred feet up in the air. But that meant we hit the desert sands with quite some force: fired like a cannonball into the sand. The impact knocked us all senseless for several minutes, until…

'Wakey wakey! Rise and shine!' The voice of SKP was the first thing we heard, laughing and singing and sounding very pleased with itself indeed. 'We made it! We're all in one piece – just about! Calloo-callay! Hurray! Hurray! And all thanks to me! SKP!'

I sat up and saw that Peter was lying crumpled. Karl the cat-dog was excitedly licking his face.

'Lora, are you okay…?' Toaster helped me up. He had a new jagged crack in the glass panel of his face.

'How's Peter?'

'I-I'm okay…'

The pod was half-buried in glittering ruby-red sand.

It had burst and split open like a piece of fruit flung to the ground, and we could see the burning red skies through wrenched-apart metal.

There was a hissing of steam and a piercing klaxon going off.

'Aha! Oh dear! Oh, SKP! Esss-Kaaay-Peeee!' the computer voice shrilled. 'Erm, we've got a problem, dear little occupants. Dear little souls whom I have just rescued!'

'What is it?' I shouted.

'I am afraid I am about to explode! Do excuse me! Please, do evacuate with all due haste, my friends. I am so very sorry our acquaintance must finish with such rudeness and the most unforgivable deadliness on my part, but it really can't be helped! My nuclear engines are going kaput and I'm about to go off with a great big bang!'

SKP sounded horribly upset, more for the danger she was putting us in than what was about to happen to her.

We were on our feet in a flash, disentangling ourselves from the safety harnesses and clambering towards the jagged opening in the pod. 'But what can we do to help you?' Peter asked, soft-hearted as ever. 'We can't let you be blown apart!'

'Ah, my dear young sir! My job here on this horrible planet of Mars is over if I have saved two human lives. What more was I created for?'

'SKP is right,' Toaster said. 'That was her function.'

'I must insist you get out to safety right now,' she

squealed. 'Seriously, in a matter of seconds I am going to go sky-high!'

'How many?' Peter asked.

'Erm … *fifty-seven*! Everything is overloading. I've got fiery particles coursing through every chamber and tube. All my remaining fuel is … ooohhh! I'm about to go supernova, or something rather like it! Please, my new friends … hurry to safety!'

I didn't need telling a third or a fourth time.

Luckily, somehow, the hole punched in the side of SKP was big enough for us to squeeze out of. Good job, too. The actual hatch looked buckled and ruined: we'd never have got out that way.

'Peter, Karl … Toaster … come on!'

'Wait.' Peter was examining a bank of instruments by the ruined hatchway. He had slowed right down and was considering the faltering lights carefully. His face was lit up a sickly yellow. 'I've seen something like this before. My music teacher was a similar design.'

'Really?'

Now the noise around us was as fierce and scary as anything aboard the *Vonnegut* had been. The metal skin around us was vibrating, as if SKP was about to shake itself apart.

'Got it!' Peter shouted, with a grin. 'Found it!' And with that, he reached out with one finger and clicked a certain switch.

A little door opened, and inside it was a slim plastic cassette. This Peter plucked out and stowed away inside his coveralls.

'Is that it?' I said.

'SKP is an escapee!' he laughed. 'Along with us. Now, come on, before the pod bursts into flaming smithereens!'

Then we were bundling our way through the jagged gap in the pod, into the searing brightness of the valley. Again, Toaster had a bit of a struggle getting his bigger bulk through the aperture.

We kept running and didn't look back.

We just about made it to a bank of dunes before the pod self-destructed.

The explosion was even louder and more violent than we'd anticipated. It rocked the valley, sending cascades of boulders tumbling down the mountainsides and causing the ground to tremble beneath us.

'Wow!' I heard Peter yelling. It must have been loud, because we all went quite deaf for a few moments as we hugged each other in the safety of the dunes. We were glad to be alive.

Eventually, we peeked out to see the pod had gone, leaving only a crater where it had been.

And there, hovering above the valley, was the gigantic form of the *Vonnegut*.

'Oh, my,' said Toaster. 'Just look at that.'

It was like a vast silver fish, suspended way above us.

I found it hard to believe that we had been aboard that thing, less than ten minutes ago. It seemed too unlikely to be true.

At least the deadly lasers had stopped firing all over the place. Maybe – hopefully – Ma Taproot had exerted some control over the situation. Or perhaps Arnold was conserving energy and preparing for his next destructive onslaught.

'What now?' asked Peter.

I was staring into the distance.

At the southern end of the valley there was a cloud of dusty exhaust fumes approaching through the air. Billowing and scarlet.

'Is that a storm?' Peter asked.

He didn't know desert signs like I did. That was no storm coming our way.

'It's the vehicle,' Toaster said. 'The one that the Ancient detected. It's heading towards us.'

I was squinting like mad. 'What kind of thing *is* that?'

As it came closer, and we could make out more details, both Peter and I realised that we had indeed seen something like this before.

We had seen it in the private museum of Professor Swiftnick.

It was a Celestial Omnibus.

22

It really looked like something that had come from another planet, just as much as the *Vonnegut* did, hovering way above our heads.

I set off at a run to meet the Celestial Omnibus.

'Lora, wait!' Peter ran after me, with Karl barking at his heels.

'You're right to be cautious,' Toaster told him. 'We don't know who's on that bus. It could be anyone. Lora!' He set off at a run too.

But there was no stopping me. Deep down, I knew who was aboard that Celestial Omnibus.

Brilliant golden wheels flashed and whizzed around as the bus soared twenty feet in the air. The sides of the bus were painted pink and green, with the name of the company picked out in large, friendly writing: *The Celestial Omnibus Company*. In places there were dents and pockmarks in the metal, where the bus had been caught in meteor storms or had been scoured by the space winds.

I ran till my breath was ragged.

Then I stood right in the path of the speeding vehicle. They could see me, I knew.

'Professor Swiftnick!' I yelled at the top of my voice.

'Lora!' Toaster was horrified. He thought I'd get myself knocked down.

'Get back, Lora!' Peter yelled.

I knew they weren't about to run me down. I laughed and pointed at the silver ship hovering above our heads. 'Look, Professor! We dug up one of the old Starships for you!'

I think Peter thought I had gone mad. Couldn't I see that we were in danger? Caught between these powerful vessels?

But the omnibus slowed down and came to a halt of grinding gears and gruff old engines. Plumes of dust and diesel fumes rolled around us, making Karl cough.

I could see the old professor sitting proudly behind the wheel of the bus. All dressed up in his finest clothes. He was staring in amazement at me, and at the *Vonnegut* looming above the valley.

And beside him? Standing right beside the old professor?

It was my da.

'Oh my!' said Peter, starting to laugh with delight.

The doors of the bus flew open with a hissing noise. They folded back like magic.

A broad, tall, bearded figure came hastening out of there like they weren't opening fast enough. He crossed those few yards of sand as fast as he could, limping and lurching towards me. Suddenly my da was hugging me like he hadn't seen me in ten years.

My face was pressed against those soft bristles of his beard as he sobbed out loud and didn't care who heard him.

My feelings were something I usually tried to keep inside, but he was hugging me so hard they all came squeezing out. Soon I was crying, too, squashed up in his arms against his rough waistcoat and his soft white shirt.

'I'll never go away like that again,' I said. 'I promise, Da, I'll never run off again on some adventure without telling you. But we thought you'd be better at home … and then you were ill! I saw you! Were you really ill?'

He put me down at last and took a good long look at me. 'Yeah, I had a fever for a while. But I got better. Old Man Horace brought me medicine and soup and stuff. I was sure glad to get over it.'

Now other figures were emerging from the colourful omnibus.

'Al!' My brother was stepping shyly out of the bus, blinking in the sun. He looked so much older and more grown up somehow, and yet it had only been a matter of weeks or months, hadn't it?

He even let me hug him. 'Thank you,' I told him. 'For believing me. And for helping.'

Professor Swiftnick hung back warily. He knew I didn't like him, and he knew I had no reason to trust him. But he was the owner of this vehicle. He had brought my family here. He was clearly trying to make amends, and he had succeeded.

Solemnly I reached out to shake his hand. Peter and Karl hung back: they would never trust the professor who had once taken them both prisoner.

And then…

'Lora! Lora, my dear! Here we are again!' Barbra's jolly voice burst through the air as she clambered awkwardly down from the bus. The bulk of the vending machine could barely get out through those narrow doors. There was no stopping her, though, and her delight was plain for everyone to hear as she came lumbering up to me.

We hugged, even though she couldn't feel anything at all, and her glass panel pressed painfully against me.

Then she looked up and squealed. 'Toaster … Toaster, my dear!'

The sunbed stepped forward smartly, as if standing to attention. 'Barbra. How very nice to see you again.'

We all watched them, as if waiting for them to hug each other. But of course they wouldn't. They couldn't. Barbra inched forward, but Toaster remained still.

'I am so, so glad to see you,' Barbra smiled. Then she started rummaging around at once for snacks and drinks for everyone.

'I suggest we find some shade,' Peter said. 'And perhaps we should get away from the *Vonnegut*…'

The professor shielded his eyes with both hands and

stared in wonderment at the Starship. 'How does it simply hang there? Like a beautiful joke? Like an elegant proposition? Something grand and inexplicable from out of the past?' He was quivering with excitement, his jowls shaking with emotion. 'Don't you understand, my friends? This is living history. This is perfection. It is pure magic!'

Then that greedy, crafty look crept over his whole countenance. The professor I knew of old was returning.

'And I must know more. I want to learn about it. I want to get aboard. I want it … I want it more than anything…'

'We've just escaped from it, actually,' said Peter happily. 'We've just flown down in an escape pod, which exploded shortly afterwards. And, really, I'm not sure you'd want to be up there just now. The *Vonnegut* is in the hands of the Ancients. We've only just managed to get away. They want to revive all ten Starships that are buried here.'

No sooner were we aboard the omnibus than there came a series of explosions and the bus rocked and bounced on its chassis.

'What is that?' Barbra cried.

Peter was peering out of the windows. His face was bathed in the eerie glow of lasers. The bus shuddered and lurched again. The noises were horrible: savage beams crackling against the sides of the omnibus.

'I should have stayed…' moaned Toaster.

'We're shielded, it's all right…' shouted Swiftnick. 'For now, but we're just a sitting duck here.' He hurried down the aisle to the driver's cab. 'The shields won't last forever. Not against the firepower of a whole Starship.'

The next few moments were pretty hairy. The blue and green laser bolts went skidding by the windows.

'Oh, Toaster,' Barbra was shouting at the top of her voice. 'Why are they doing this? Why do they hate us so much?'

'They don't mean to. They can't control the ships and the technology. But I can,' said Toaster.

'Really?' said Barbra, full of admiration.

'We won't let you go to them,' I told him. 'You belong with us.'

At this moment the engines roared into life underneath us.

The Celestial Omnibus gave a huge and hungry furious cry.

'Hold on tight!' Da yelled. 'This thing bucks around like an unbroken burden beast!'

Quite suddenly the bus leapt further into the air.

'It's wonderful!' Peter shouted, half laughing, half amazed. 'What a fantastic machine!'

It truly was. I thought about how it had travelled all the way from Earth to Mars, there and back, carrying sixty passengers at a time.

It was a kind of impossible machine, really. It looked so

mundane and so unimpressive next to the silvery bulk of the *Vonnegut* and those other grand Starships. And yet, two hundred years before, this omnibus and others like it were ferrying folk secretly through space. And now, undeterred, the little bus was speeding through the air, weaving and dodging laser fire and the jagged, deadly walls of the valley.

We all clung on as hard as we could.

'Just get us away from here,' Da bellowed at Swiftnick. 'Cut out the fancy flying manoeuvres and the showing off… Get us to safety!'

'This isn't showing off!' the professor yelled. His hands were clamped to the wheel and he was veering us about crazily. 'I'm trying to get us away. What do you think I'm doing?'

I shook my head. 'I know you won't let us die, Professor. Not here. Not like this. You're too keen on self-preservation…'

There was a volley of green laser fire just then – the most sustained and accurate blast so far – and it shook the omnibus to the core. The engines faltered and sputtered and went silent.

We were several hundred metres up in the air by then. If we started to fall we were all doomed.

'Professor…' Da shouted out, and started hauling himself down the aisle, grabbing handholds as he went, lurching towards the cab.

Everything seemed to be in agonising slow motion.

I caught Peter's eye and he looked shocked. Frozen at the window. We were going to plummet back to the valley floor and we were all going to die.

This was it. After everything. We had run out of luck at last.

But I had forgotten how, in a crisis, I could always rely on Da.

With a great cry of rage he flung himself at the professor, and dropped his whole bodily weight onto the omnibus controls. There was a flash and a shower of sparks as the damaged control column came unstuck.

Swiftnick bellowed. 'You've done it, sir. You've…!'

Da ignored him, seizing control of the steering wheel. The omnibus turned wildly about in mid-air. There was a horrific screech as we whirled about and accelerated through the sky, putting as much distance between us and the firepower of the *Vonnegut* as we possibly could.

As soon as I could get back on my feet I was running down that aisle.

'You saved us! Da, you've saved us!'

'Not bad, eh?' he grinned through his beard, which looked more bristly than ever, all bushed out in the electrified air. Then he whipped off his hat and screamed with triumph and delight.

'We're running out of fuel,' Swiftnick pointed out. 'Look, let me navigate. I know where we can go.' He started clicking away at the navigational controls as my da steered the way through the skies and we glided peacefully away from the Valley of the Starships.

'Let's just get right away from the *Vonnegut*,' I said.

'It doesn't appear to be following us,' observed Toaster. 'I imagine the Ancients are still struggling to discover how to work the controls. They'll find it all much harder without my help…'

'Where are you taking us?' Da asked Swiftnick.

'To the closest settlement,' said the professor tersely. 'Back to Ruby's town.'

23

But to get to Ruby's town we had to fly over the swamplands first. Peter and I gazed out of the windows at that vast jungle expanse. We were amazed that we had ever ventured into it, let alone emerged from there alive.

As Da steered the Celestial Omnibus through the misty skies my brother Al was telling the tale of how he got everyone together in the City Inside. Barbra made a few interjections, filling in details that he missed and exclaiming now and then over how brave everyone had been.

Al seemed like a different boy altogether from the one I had last seen in the City. Back then he had been almost taken over by the Graveley family and that horrible, snooty daughter of theirs. It turned out that those scales had finally fallen from his eyes and he'd realised that the Graveleys were only interested in themselves and feathering their own plush nests.

One evening, forced to accompany them to the Grand Opera, Al had snuck away from their party and caught up with the professor. The old man was revelling in his newfound celebrity – as the hero returned from disaster and adventure in the wilderness. Barbra, too, had had her photo taken for the newspapers – heralded as a courageous survivor of an ill-fated expedition – and that night she was with Swiftnick at the opera.

'We had a box of our own and everything,' Barbra sighed. 'And I had stocked champagne and chocolates, but no sooner were we settled down for the performance, than this young fellow comes dashing in, telling us that he was no better than a prisoner of the Graveley family. He told us how they wouldn't even let him visit his poor father, whom he just knew was lying ill in bed.'

Al was looking at me. 'Just like you told me, Lora. Like you said in your telepathic message. I knew it was all true. I believed in you. And I knew I had to fetch help in order to make sure Da was okay.'

I flushed at this. How much had we bickered with each other as kids and in the City Inside? To find out that, when the chips were down, Al believed in me was a wonderful feeling.

'We weren't sure the message had really got through,' I said. 'It was the machinery of the Ancients we were using. The same machinery they've got Ma and Hannah hooked up to…'

'Well, you surely got through to me, and Professor Swiftnick was fascinated to hear about it. We crept out of the Grand Opera House and hurried away to his carriage. Then we went rushing through the snowy streets all the

246

way to Bolingbroke District. And I can't tell you how great it felt to be away at last from the Graveleys.'

'The poor boy was shaking,' said Barbra. 'He was quite upset.'

'I was worried about Da,' said Al. 'From the way you'd described your vision of him, Lora, it was like he must be at death's door.'

Al and the others had gone running through the dark alleyways and up the metal fire escapes, until they came to Da's flat at the very top. There Da lay, just as I had seen him, feverish and sick. At first he thought he was hallucinating when Al and the professor and Barbra came bursting into his room.

'All he needed was a little feeding and watering,' said Barbra. 'We soon got him back on his feet. And then there was no stopping him. He wanted to know about everything that had happened. He demanded to know the latest about you, Lora, and your ma and sister and grandma. He limps around a bit, but he's quite a forceful chap, isn't he? He turned on the professor and scolded him for leaving you all out here in the terrible wilderness. And oh, I must admit, I did feel ashamed, too. I feel I should have insisted on accompanying you and Peter and Toaster into the swamplands. I'm sure I could have been of some help.'

Barbra peered out of the bus windows at the leafy canopy far below and shuddered.

'Don't worry about it,' I told her. 'I'm glad you were in the City, helping Al and Da for me.'

'So, the next thing,' Al continued, 'was Da demanding that the professor come up with a way to get us all into the wilderness so we could find you. Well, of course, he didn't have a second Sky Saucer up his sleeve. He'd put all his resources into creating the first. But what he did have was something very special, hidden away deep in his museum. Something very old and unique.'

'The Celestial Omnibus!' I said. 'But who would have thought it could ever fly again?' I recalled seeing it myself in Swiftnick's private museum, and being amazed by its gaudily painted shell. It was an astonishing piece of ancient history, and yet here it was.

'It was Da, of course,' said Al proudly. 'He got it going again, didn't he? You know that he can fix anything mechanical, our da.'

We all turned to look at him then, up at the front of the bus, wrestling with the vast steering wheel, piloting us through the dense purple clouds.

'We're making an unscheduled stop before Ruby's town!' Toaster announced. He came down the aisle with a determined look on his cracked glass countenance. 'We have detected some strange activity in the jungle below.'

I was on my feet in a flash, and hurrying up to the driver's cab. 'What sort of strange activity?'

'Servo-Furnishings,' said Toaster. 'Also, there is an unusual energy signature emerging from deep underground…'

It felt good to arrive in Bandit Town aboard the bus, and with some back-up. We hadn't seen the Servo-Furnishings since they'd been thrown out of the Underworld and it was hard to know how they would treat our arrival.

The Celestial Omnibus crashed through the jungle canopy, landing with a hefty thump and bringing down a shower of leaves.

We were surrounded at once by gawping Servos. They held up their ramshackle weapons and stared at us incredulously. It was the same rabble of cabinets and refrigerators Peter and I had seen before. The Servo with the green trumpet mouth was hallooing madly again.

Professor Swiftnick gasped at the sight of them all. 'They're prehistoric! Just look at them! Precious antiques!'

'Are they dangerous?' Da asked.

'Not while I'm around,' said Toaster. 'They seem to worship me.'

'I'm not surprised, Toaster,' said Barbra. 'So they should.'

The sunbed darted her a look. Was she being sarcastic? But Barbra was never sarcastic. She always said exactly what she meant.

The doors of the omnibus opened and out we shuffled.

'Uh, Mr Robinson, sir,' said Peter, clutching Karl to his chest. 'You may have to brace yourself for a big surprise.'

I knew exactly what he meant. Perhaps I should have said something to prepare Da, too, but before I could there was a stirring in the crowd of Servo-Furnishings. Out came a figure in battered space fatigues and a cracked helmet, accompanied by Grandma in her oldest cardigan. She was looking just as surprised as anyone by the arrival of the Celestial Omnibus in the middle of Bandit Town.

'Ma!' yelled Da. He pushed through the crowd, limping heavily on his damaged leg. The Servos drew apart and we all watched as he seized the tiny woman and whirled her through the air.

'Where have you been?' he demanded. 'What on Mars were you doing, zooming off into the wilderness aboard a flying saucer?'

'I was looking for your wife and youngest daughter, as it happens,' she answered huffily, even as he was spinning her joyously around. 'We've been through all kinds of tribulations like you wouldn't believe. Oh, do put me down, Edward, or else I'll be sick.' He did so and she started squawking. 'Edward! Edward! Oh, my son! I've missed you so much!'

To my surprise, Grandma burst into noisy and messy tears.

Da hugged her tight again. When she looked up at last she fixed her eyes blearily on the rest of us.

'Al! You're here! And Lora! And … Toaster! So, you've

come back to me, too, have you? After you ran out and abandoned me here?'

Toaster became very solemn. 'I apologise, Margaret Robinson. But my place was with Lora. We had a quest to carry out.'

Grandma pulled a ferocious face at us all. 'Some quest! And did you succeed? Just what did you get up to, eh?'

Barbra spoke up chirpily. 'It wasn't a complete success, by all accounts. But seemingly, they've managed to find the ten Starships from planet Earth and install the gestalt mind of the Ancients of Mars inside the blue-crystal circuits of the Starship *Vonnegut*. Hello, everyone – I'm Barbra! I'm a vending machine!'

Barbra's honesty could sometimes be annoying.

My great-uncle Thomas took off his glass helmet. His already wrinkled face was crumpled even further in dismay. 'You've given the Ancients control over the Starships?'

'Er, yes,' I said. 'Sort of. It all happened quite quickly … All they're interested in is the power of those Starships. They want to get up among the stars.'

'And now you've gone and given that power to them,' said Uncle Thomas gloomily.

Uncle Thomas and Grandma could see that we were all worn out and not fit for a discussion so they led us into Bandit Town. Da was amazed to meet his long-lost and legendary uncle for the first time, and learned how

Thomas had vanished into the swamps with renegade Servos all those many years ago. Meanwhile Grandma had hold of Al and was hugging him like she wanted to squish him to death.

I didn't know how to tell Da or Grandma that we had found Ma and Hannah but left them behind once again. I didn't know what to say.

Professor Swiftnick talked to Grandma and she thanked him for bringing her family to her in the Celestial Omnibus, surprising him – and everyone else – by putting her arms around him and giving him a kiss on both bright red, whiskery cheeks.

'I knew you weren't an outright crazy-assed villain,' she cackled. 'And you've gone and proved it, Professor Swiftnick. You've done a good thing today!'

The professor beamed at this and drank the home-brewed bark rum that the Servos were passing round.

There was an impromptu celebration that night in Bandit Town. There was raucous music and the food that was brought out was more appetising than what they offered us last time we were there, before they made me a prisoner. Or perhaps we were just hungrier.

Darkness encroached and glowing lanterns were lit. There was laughter and singing of old Earth songs, but I found that I couldn't relax.

'I'm worried,' I told Peter. 'The clock is still ticking, isn't it? We can't forget. The Ancients are aboard the *Vonnegut*.

They'll try to revive the other Starships, too. We don't know what they might do next.'

'I think we'll be okay for tonight,' said Peter. 'You know, you should really take the chance to relax. We're among friends.'

I was amazed by his complacency. 'Are we?' I hissed at him. I watched the Servos beetling about amongst the trees and between the buildings. Toaster was regaling a group of them with tales of his recent adventures. Grandma was dancing cheek to cheek with Swiftnick, moving to the crackling strains of some old jazz music.

'You have to start trusting people at some point,' Peter said. 'You can't run forever.' Karl yapped at me, as if to underline what Peter was saying. I patted Karl and smiled at Peter.

'Yeah, I know. Let me get my head together. You go and enjoy yourselves…'

Peter looked at me worriedly. 'Are you sure?'

'I'm okay! Honestly!'

I wandered alone to the fringes of Bandit Town, where the light was dimmer and the music and shouting faded into the background. I ducked under a fringe of dense leaves and ventured into the dark forest beyond. I liked the feeling of merging with the darkness. It was cool and strange and suited my frame of mind.

I only wanted a little peace. I only wanted some thinking time on my own.

But I hadn't wandered for long before I realised that there were eyes suspended in the darkness, and they were staring straight at me.

They were large and bright. Golden-green in colour and horribly veiny. There were six, seven, eight, nine of them ... and more! Each one was at the end of a swaying, dripping tentacle.

Goomba ... Goomba had found me again!

24

His huge form came lumbering out of the darkness. It seemed a lifetime since we had last met the guardian of the swamp. I'd almost forgotten how terrifying and huge he was, though I did remember the brackish, horrible stench of the bog that he brought with him.

Now I was standing before him again and his voice buffeted like a hot wind.

'Lora Robinson! You did exactly what Goomba warned you not to!'

He sounded like our schoolteacher back on the prairie, the way she called me out by my whole name, always when I'd been caught doing something wrong.

'I'm s-sorry,' I stammered.

'You went ahead and you woke up the Sleepers!'

The voice of Goomba was thunderous. Surely everyone back in Bandit Town would hear him yelling at me, no matter how loud their partying was?

'I had no choice about that,' I said. 'We went into the Underworld to find my ma and my sister, and the Sleepers were awake and they were waiting for us. The Ancients already had us in mind as part of their plan, I think. They knew we were coming to see them. I think it's why they took Ma and Hannah prisoner in the first place.'

Goomba sighed and swamp water drooled out of his mildewy lips. 'For so long these swamplands have been very quiet,' he boomed. 'They have been safe and boring and dull. And what's happened recently? You and your friends and family and robots have gone and ruined the peace.'

'Like I say, I'm sorry,' I said. 'But I had to do what I could.'

I stared back into his many golden eyes as they waved at the end of their stalks.

'All I wanted to do was get my family back together. I had to rescue each and every one of them but I'm sorry if that disturbed your peace and quiet.'

Goomba shook his huge head. 'No, no, no! It was much too dull before. You've no idea how boring it is hanging about in a swamp, trying to be quiet when you're as big and as noisy as I am. You shook things up and brought change and excitement. And now the Sleepers are awake and perhaps that's just as it should be. The Ancient Ones have emerged from their slumbers and they have vacated their labyrinth. There is no one for me to be guardian of anymore.'

'They've left the Underworld? All of them?'

Goomba nodded, spraying swamp water everywhere. 'It is so. They are going elsewhere. They are heading into the stars.'

I felt ashamed. 'Yeah, we kind of helped them out with that a bit. Maybe a mistake on our part… But, listen. The labyrinth is really empty now?'

'The Underworld beneath us is so very quiet,' sighed Goomba.

'In that case,' I said, 'my mother and sister – they're down there alone in that place. Down in the labyrinth.'

'I suppose they will be,' said Goomba gloomily. 'But even if the Ancients are gone, I believe their machinery will rumble on for many years automatically. It will keep the air clean and your relatives will be given fresh water and food each day, and there will be distracting pictures for them to look at. They will still be quite happy down there, even if the Ancients have all departed to find a new home among the stars… Yes, I'm sure they'll be safe. I'm mostly sure. I think I'm sure.'

Now Goomba was looking up at the creaking canopy of dark leaves. Only a glimmer of silky night could be seen through the jagged gaps. There was only the slightest smattering of stars to gaze at. I suddenly felt upset for the swamp guardian. His only job had ever been to ensure that the Ancient Ones were never disturbed. They had left without warning him. What was Goomba going to do now?

I made a snap decision. 'Will you help me?'

'Me?' he frowned massively. 'Me, help you, Lora Robinson? But … but … aren't you terrified of me?'

I stared up into his gnarled and puzzled face and wondered.

'Not really,' I told him. 'I'm sorry. I know I'm meant to be. And you're monstrous and all the rest of it. But I'm not scared of you like I'm supposed to be. I guess I was a little the first time we met but I reckon you're probably okay, really.'

The many eyes quivered at the ends of their stalks. He was astonished.

'So, will you help me?'

'Help you do what?' he thundered, suspiciously, but he was intrigued, too, I could tell. He was pleased by this notion of not necessarily being the scariest being I had ever encountered.

I explained my idea and, to my surprise, Goomba agreed.

'I've lived in this swamp for hundreds of years and I've had my fill. My two highlights in recent times are when you've turned up, ruining the peace. No one else has even dared to come near! Let alone spoken to me, or stood up to me!'

I let the swamp guardian pick me up and place me gently on his back. Then he surged out of the sepulchral waters and moved with surprising speed and agility between the trees. His flesh was hard and knotted. It was like sitting up in the boughs of a tree. I just hoped he remembered I was perched up there on his shoulders.

Soon he announced: 'Behold! The entrance to the Underworld!'

Yes: just as it had been before, when we were fleeing from Uncle Thomas and his Bandit Servos. I wondered briefly whether this was a wise course of action, returning to this perilous place in the company of a terrifying primordial beast, without having told anyone else where I was off to – but it was too late for qualms now.

Goomba heaved himself up to the entrance and started pulling away great chunks of soggy earth and matted vegetation. 'It's all got a bit overgrown,' he said, hefting and hewing as he went.

Soon the entranceway was large enough to admit him.

We descended those smooth, sandy steps. The tunnels swept ever downwards and, as we went, Goomba grew quieter. He was nervous, I think, at being so far from his natural element. For a long time the only sound was the squelching thump of his huge feet.

All the way down his swaying eyes lit our way. Sitting on his shoulders I was treated to a terrific close-up view of those hyro-griffics which were painted on the walls.

Once Goomba paused thoughtfully and lifted a creaking finger to point at a certain illustration. It was a gaudy and crude representation of the swamp beast himself, and he was surrounded by beings who looked just like Arnold. Small, harmless-seeming creatures. Ma Taproot stood with them and had her arms raised imperiously. She was clearly commanding Goomba as he sat there up to his chest in the turgid green waters.

'That was my special day,' he said sadly. 'When they told me what my destiny was and what I must do.'

'How long ago was that, Goomba?' I asked him.

'Too long,' he said, sadly. 'And they left me there, in the swamp. And, I suppose, they forgot about me.'

He stirred himself and off we went again. Down and down the winding steps to the Underworld.

At last we came to that underground expanse in the centre of which grew a tree with white leaves that had never seen the light of day. Its leaves trembled and whispered as before, swaying in a non-existent breeze.

'Can you hear that?' Goomba asked, setting me down on the pale sandy floor of the cavern.

I listened hard.

'I hoped it would be different,' he moaned. 'I thought everything might continue as it was, even in the Ancients' absence. But I have a horrible feeling … that something is happening to the labyrinth.'

Now that he mentioned it, there was indeed a strange crackling sound. It was all around us. It reminded me of the noise just before a sandstorm on the prairie, when all the dunes were about to be shifted and swept into new configurations.

'I fear that the whole place is going to collapse soon,' whispered Goomba. His voice seemed to go deeply down into the very roots of the place. 'Now that the Ancients have abandoned this place, it is starting to fall. Perhaps your relatives won't be so safe here, after all...'

My heart ached for the gentle swamp beast. He stood there looking at the pale tree in the centre of the cavern and I had never seen a lonelier-looking creature. He looked like he didn't have a clue what he was supposed to do.

25

A female voice called out: 'Not yet! We haven't quite gone yet!'

It was coming from the tree and I realised at once who it must be. Ma Taproot was back in her old body with its voluminous clothes and wild hair, with a ragged shawl wrapped around her shoulders. She was coming down the wooden steps that wound round her tree, carrying a heavy cardboard box in her arms.

She beamed as she approached us. 'Hello, Lora, dear. And Goomba – how very nice to see you again. I'd forgotten all about you, I'm afraid. How terrible it would have been to leave you languishing in that swamp. Guarding this old place, even after we've all slipped away...'

Goomba's eyestalks quivered with suppressed rage, and his glowing eyes wept slime. Yet he kept his voice soft and respectful for the old lady: 'You wouldn't have left Goomba alone, being the guardian of nothing? You wouldn't have left him watching over an empty Underworld?'

She laughed throatily. 'Oh dear. Yes, that sounds awful, doesn't it? How very thoughtless of us. And I suppose we have been dreadful, haven't we? So caught up in our dreams of infinite knowledge and enlightenment and attaining our next state of being … we never gave much consideration to a swamp beast like you. You served us so faithfully, too, down all these many years.'

Goomba hung his heavy head.

'Still,' Ma Taproot went on. 'You did find Lora Robinson, and I'm sure she'll look after you. She's very good with waifs and strays and cast-offs. She collects them up, don't you, dear? You've done it all your life.'

I stared at her. It was hard to be angry with her, the way she burbled on in such a friendly seeming manner. But inside I was seething about all the danger we had faced. It was all down to her and her ancient people.

'We've come for my ma and my sister,' I said, in a steady voice, letting her know I wasn't going to be deterred.

'Have you? That's very loyal of you,' said the old woman breezily. 'But they'd be quite safe here, I'm sure. The labyrinth and the machinery will go on running for several years yet, even without the Heart of the Ancients…'

'No,' rumbled Goomba. 'The Underworld will collapse. I can already sense it creaking and crumbling all around us. And you, Madame Taproot, are hastening along. Grabbing your precious things and your books to take with you. Hurrying away to your Starship and loading it with all your hopes. You know this Underworld is about to turn to dust and ashes.'

She looked at us sadly. 'You're right, of course. Everything here on Mars turns back into dust and ashes. The storms come down, deadly and crimson, and they whirl everything about. Nothing ever remains the same. Everything turns to bloody sand. That's how it's always been here on planet Mars. Before there were ever cities of green glass, and before there were wooden houses on the prairies. Even before there were ghosts with wings, or swamp creatures or a labyrinth with a beating heart. Mars was always in the process of churning everything into red dust, proving again and again to those who would listen that nothing ever really lasts for all time.'

She smiled at us again, wearily. Behind her, several Ancients were emerging from the tree and carrying boxes of their own in their stumpy arms.

'There are others down here, too,' I said. My voice broke. I was trying not to let my feelings show. I couldn't help it, though. I knew that Watt was gone but I still had a glimmer of hope for Sook. 'I need to know whether it's possible that Sook is still alive.'

Ma Taproot's wild white eyebrows went up in surprise. 'Oh, my dear Lora. No Martian Ghost could survive for long down here. Not so close to the Heart of Mars. Sook knew that and still she came here. The radiation from the Heart was inimical to their wings, you see. And it addled their minds. We tried to warn them. They thought that we were up to no good. In their eyes, we were never any good.

'But, in the end, all we wanted was for the humans to help us. The Martian Ghosts thought the humans needed protecting from us. We were both mistaken, in our own ways, weren't we? The humans assumed the Martian Ghosts were wicked, while thinking we were legendary beings, worthy of worship and sacrifice.

'How strange it all seems, and how unfair. But such is life, isn't it? People often get the wrong idea about others. We were all trying to do what we thought best, all for our own separate reasons.

'And so now you know the truth of it all, Lora. There really is no chance that Sook could have survived after your last meeting with her in the labyrinth. Those walls closed in on her and she breathed her last.'

Ma Taproot's words cut right into me. I knew she wasn't lying. She was even trying to be kind by telling me plainly what she believed to be true. No more lies, or secrets, or mystification.

Now Ma Taproot was standing at the bottom of the tree on the white sand. She set down her cardboard box of books and held out her palms. She spread her arms like a great, wise old bird, preparing to take flight.

'Here, my dears. Be reunited.'

I blinked – thinking I was imagining things.

Ma and Hannah stepped out from behind the old lady's bulk. Did they emerge from within her voluminous cloak, or did they step out of the tree? Either way, they were both suddenly standing there, and they were looking just as startled as I was. I cried out and ran to them.

'Lora! What's happening? Where are we now? The machinery was breaking down... The magic pictures weren't working so well ... and now ... I remember this tree ... and this woman, from before ... but, why are we here now? What's going on?'

'Ma, the rest of our family is waiting up there.'

'The rest of the family?' she said in a hollow, haunted voice.

I was worried then, staring into her pale, unhealthy-looking face. Had she lost her mind down in the labyrinth? It was never that strong, even before she had been brought to this place.

Beside Ma, Hannah was mute with resentment. She obviously hated having to leave her cell.

'Everyone is together again, in Bandit Town,' I told them. 'I've managed to bring everyone together again ... somehow. Nearly everyone. And Goomba here is part of it all, too. So, please – don't be scared of him.'

Goomba did his best to smile reassuringly at Ma and Hannah.

'Ah!' cried Ma Taproot. 'Well, I must be off. Arnold is calling from the Starship *Vonnegut* and soon we must be setting sail. Now, let me say this, Lora Robinson. Shortly we will ask for something from you. Something very important. It will be a sacrifice I hope you will be willing to make.'

My heart was thudding with dread. 'A sacrifice?'

'Not yet,' said Ma Taproot. 'I will let you all celebrate your togetherness and safety in Bandit Town. But then we will meet again tomorrow, in Ruby's Town, at the very edge of the great red prairie of Mars. All ten Starships will be revived by the Heart of Mars and we will come to you. My fleet will be ready and I will meet you and I will ask you something, and you must be ready to answer.'

'What if I don't?' I said. 'What if I don't come to the edge of the prairie?'

Ma Taproot smiled. 'Oh, I think you will. You so hate to let people down, don't you?'

Then she leaned forward and started fiddling with the box at her feet.

'Another thing. I have something here for you. Amongst these cumbersome books. Phew, you'd think they'd be lighter, somehow. But even illusory books can be heavy! Ah, here we are. Here it is. Something I found a bit broken up and left behind, down in the labyrinth. Perhaps you'd like to keep it, hmm? Maybe it could help light your way back to the surface?'

With that she lifted from the box a bent and battered table lamp. It had a wonky shade but it was the best lamp I had ever seen.

I took him in my arms.

'I am Watt! Watt I am!' the Servo cried delightedly. 'Do you remember? Do you remember me, Lora?'

267

When I looked up, Ma Taproot, her Ancients and the boxes of books had all disappeared. I was alone with Watt, Goomba, my ma and Hannah beside the pale Tree of All Knowledge – as it had once been called – and it was time to return to the others.

26

We celebrated in Bandit Town.

Imagine the faces of them all – Uncle Thomas and Grandma, Da and Al and Swiftnick and all the Servos – when I came back to town with Ma and Hannah and we were sitting on the shoulders of Goomba.

The Bandits had their own tales of Goomba, of course. Dreadful tales that they terrified each other with late at night. He was the lurking beast with ten thousand eyes who could swallow up Servos whole. He was the beast who wanted the whole swamp to keep quiet, warning of the dangers of waking the Sleepers.

But now the Sleepers had awoken after all. The Ancients were getting up and leaving. There was nothing left to fear anymore, was there?

Perhaps there never had been.

They all stared and pointed as we came crashing through the trees. What a view I had of that jungle shanty town, with everyone staring up at me in horror!

Only Peter laughed. I could pick him and Karl out easy in the crowd. He was the only one without his mouth hanging open in shock. 'Typical Lora,' he laughed, later.

Goomba carefully set us down. Me and Ma and Hannah and Watt the table lamp.

The others clustered around us, and there was the most wonderful silence. There was peace.

We were all back together again. The Robinson family was together for the first time in… Actually, no one could pinpoint exactly how long. Since we were back in the Homestead on the prairie.

Ma and Da hugged and we stood round watching them.

'Edward?' she asked tentatively. 'Is this all in my head? Is it just a magic picture?'

'What?' he smiled. 'No, no, love. This is all true. This is all real life.' He looked round ruefully at the faces surrounding them. 'Believe it or not.'

'But … I was in the Underworld…' she said.

'Not anymore,' said Da. 'We're together again. All of us are.'

They held each other like they thought they never would again.

Funny thing, our family was much bigger now than it had been before. It seemed huge, suddenly, with everyone jostling. Peter and Karl and Watt. Professor Swiftnick was standing by, warily keeping close to Grandma. Even Goomba. Uncle Thomas looked like he wasn't sure whether he had a place amongst us or not. I watched Grandma take his hand and squeeze it.

We all belonged.

Toaster and Barbra stood in the middle of us and I grinned at them both. I felt sure they knew how important they had been in getting us all here. They were never just Servos to us. They were more than mere friends. They were a part of our family.

After all these hugs and the kissing and the garbled, excited explanations, the Servo with the green trumpet started up the raucous music. The party began all over again in Bandit Town and we celebrated like crazy all night.

For that little while it was possible to blot out the thought of tomorrow, and the difficulties that it would surely bring.

The next day we travelled beyond the swamplands, heading south for the prairie. We were going to walk. Da didn't think the bus would be up to the short hop. It was going to need extensive repairs. Also, now we had Goomba with us. He was too big to climb aboard any kind of omnibus. He would lead us through his forest of vines.

We were quiet. We didn't know exactly what we were heading towards, or what kind of dangers we might have to face.

The Ancients had left their Underworld and woken the whole fleet of Starships, Ma Taproot had said.

They were coming to see us.

But first we had to make the journey back to Ruby's Town.

A little surprise was awaiting us at the fringes of the swamp. Our burden beasts, Molly and George, were grazing peacefully on the lush blue grasses. They gazed at us placidly, as if they had been expecting us to happen along any day soon to collect them. They had never been in any doubt that we'd come back this way.

We made a kind of cloak and hat using the largest leaves we could find, to cover Goomba's shoulders and head. There was a danger he'd dry out and turn to matchwood in the glaring sunlight. We never questioned that he would be coming with us.

As we set off across the red sands Ma suddenly looked frightened. 'Edward – is it all right? Are we safe now?'

Da hugged her. Ma had been shaken to the core by her experiences. She wasn't sure she could believe in everything that was happening to her now. Da held her closer.

'We're safe. And we're going home. At last, we're going home again.'

We walked and walked across the red dunes. Toaster used his charts to navigate skilfully over shifting sands, telling Al that it was down to his splendid photos of the desert that he had any maps at all. Al looked very pleased.

Barbra was very well stocked with supplies and kept us fed and watered all the way to Ruby's town.

When we came within sight of those wooden buildings, it was surprising all over again how similar they looked to the houses of Our Town, somewhere over the other side of the prairie. Men rode out to meet us on their burden beasts, guns cocked and desert goggles clamped down over their faces. They were wary and ready to fight to defend their town to the death. They looked amazed at the raggle-taggle bunch of us emerging out of the shimmering haze. Then they recognised us. They realised exactly who we were. I heard shouts go up. Cries of alarm and astonishment. We marched up to them and greeted them, and then, without breaking our step, we marched into their town.

Grandma led our procession. She bundled her cardigan around herself, clamped her hat down on her head, and walked with brisk determination. The townsfolk emerged from their homes and stores. They looked so neat and composed compared with us.

Ruby appeared all at once in our path, wearing her mannish white suit. Her expression was wary. She wasn't sure what we would say to her. How we would treat her. She held her rifle aloft. We stopped and stared at Ruby and she stared back at each of us in turn.

Once she had been so funny and friendly. Our old aunty who lived in town, and looked after her history books. Had she really forgotten all of that?

'Well, Ruby,' Grandma said. 'Here we all are. Back in your town. We did everything we said we were gonna do. Everyone has been rescued and everyone is here now. And what have you got to say about that?'

It was a tense moment. We could feel the whole town watching and bracing itself.

Ruby spoke. 'You met the Ancient Ones?'

This was my cue to step forward. 'Yes! I met them. And so did Ma and Hannah and Toaster, and Peter and Karl, and Watt. We spent time in their Underworld and we went to the very Heart of Mars.'

Ruby went about as red as her name. 'But … they never listened to me. They never heeded my prayers. They never said a single word to me, even though we worshipped them so piously. They never came to us. Tell me … please, Lora, tell me … what are our Gods actually like?'

'They aren't gods, for one thing,' I told her. 'They are just very old and very different from us. That doesn't make them gods, you know.'

Ruby looked at me like she thought I was making fun of her and being cruel.

'Listen,' I said. 'This is your chance. Today, this very afternoon, we are going to see them again, one final time. At the very edge of the prairie. If you declare a truce with us – shelter us and feed us and treat us as your guests – and if we can carry on in peace together as good neighbours ought, then you can come along with us and meet the Ancients. What do you say?'

The old woman looked near to tears. 'They are coming … *here*?'

27

It was less than three hours later.

We made quite a big group. Almost the whole town rode out with us on burden beasts and hovercarts. Our party ranged in age from Grandma down to Hannah, and in size from Watt up to Goomba.

We were quiet and careful as we approached: not knowing quite what to expect.

'Is this the place, do you think?' Da asked me.

I nodded.

We sat down in the searing sunlight and waited.

Toaster let us know that something was happening in the skies.

'Here they come,' he said.

Even as he announced the Starships, we could hear them approach. The ground quaked beneath us. There was a deep vibration in our bones. We stood up and shielded our eyes, staring into the light. We craned our necks and held our breath.

'Oh, look!' Peter gasped.

Ten Starships. Each a different size and shape. Each one a different colour. Pink and gold and black, heliotrope and red. None of them really matched another, but somehow they all looked perfect together, moving in careful formation.

The smallest and shabbiest craft was the *Vonnegut*, and it flew at the head of the fleet.

It was terrifyingly obvious that we were in huge danger. Now they had us arrayed before them. We were defenceless. They could let loose with the laser fire. All that pent-up lightning that had lain dormant in the bellies of the Starships: so easy to let it loose and wipe us out.

Professor Swiftnick fell to his knees. He was seeing his wildest imaginings coming to life before his very eyes. He cried out hoarsely. Here was an idea too big to grasp, too vast to own or contain. All he could do was cry out in joy.

The townsfolk followed his lead, and so did Ruby. They all fell to the dusty ground and shouted out together incoherently as the Starships slid closer to us.

The ships filled up the whole sky.

Grandma and Thomas were crying and holding each other, like people seeing their childhood home once more. Toaster stood up, courageous and proud. His cracked face gleamed with delight.

Then, all at once, the Starships halted in mid-air. They froze silently, perhaps half a mile above us.

'*Lora?*'

It was Arnold's voice in my head. Gentle, like when we had first met him, down in the labyrinth.

I blinked and saw that there was a small cluster of figures just ahead of us. They hadn't been there moments before.

Peter squinted through the delicate heat haze. 'It's the Ancients. Ma Taproot and Arnold and others…'

'I have to go to them,' I said. 'I promised I would.'

A hand reached out and grasped my arm and I was surprised to see it was Ma. 'Y-you aren't leaving us, are you, Lora?'

'No! No, of course not.'

Her face relaxed and she smiled. 'Don't leave us again,' she said, and Da took hold of her and nodded at me.

Only I could go and talk with the Ancients now. I didn't know what they wanted. What if they started demanding something I couldn't give?

As I stepped forward and walked towards them I realised that everyone here was dependent on me and how I handled this moment. I walked alone to meet the Ancient Ones in the shadow of the Starships.

'My dear,' Ma Taproot smiled, and hugged me. The Ancients reached out with their little hands to pat me.

Ma Taproot smelled of honey and lilac.

Arnold seemed ashamed. 'I'm so sorry … I lost control of the ship and its weapons, the last time we were together.' He blinked his black button eyes at me. 'I'd never been in charge of a powerful Starship before. They are quite complicated, all the controls. I'm not as good with all of that as Toaster is.'

'You got them all flying again,' I said, staring up at the scarred undersides of the ships. The air wavered with the heat of their engines. It was like looking up at a whole city, suspended over our heads.

'Ah, yes,' smiled Ma Taproot. 'It took quite a lot of effort, really. But once your brilliant Toaster had set the blue crystals singing deep inside the machine, we could manage the rest. We could coax them into life. And that brings me rather neatly to our reason for asking to meet with you here, before we leave this world.'

I steeled myself. Now I knew what they were going to ask. In the past few moments I had guessed.

'You want him, don't you? You need his help, and his blue-crystal mind.'

She smiled. 'Would he come with us, do you think? If we asked him?'

'To explore the galaxy?' I laughed. 'You'll have to ask him yourself, but I think I know the answer to that one.'

I turned to look back at my family and friends.

Toaster was already making his way towards us, shambling over the dust and sand. His logic circuits had made the leap and he had realised what the Ancients were after.

Only Toaster could fuse his own mind with those of the ten Starships and take them back out into the universe. Only he could make sure that all that power didn't destroy itself.

It was his destiny, and he of all creatures knew that. It was his chance to explore and to learn things that no one else knew anything about.

'Here comes Toaster!' Ma Taproot hooted. She shouted to him: 'Won't you come with us, my dear sir? Won't you journey with us to the stars?'

Toaster stopped in his tracks. 'I … cannot leave Mars.'

Ma Taproot's face fell. The Ancients clustered around her, looking shocked, whispering amongst themselves. 'What did he say? What was that? Can he really mean it?'

'Toaster?' I went to him and he was looking his most solemn. He was quite still, staring at the ground. He was deliberately not looking up at the amazing Starships.

'Toaster?' I put my hand on his glass chest and I could feel it trembling, as if all the mechanical parts inside him were shaking themselves loose. He was raging with indecision inside.

'I will not leave the Robinson family,' he said, in a strange, cracked voice.

'I think you must,' I told him.

'Lora, I have very rarely failed in my programming. Only when my mind was tampered with, have I deviated from the task I took on all those years ago. I am the protector of Margaret Estelle Robinson, your grandma, and everyone in her family. All the Robinsons are my reason for living. I am your Servo.'

'I know that, Toaster. We all know that. You have been

the best Servo-Furnishing anyone has ever had. You've been much more than that.'

By now the Ancients were talking amongst themselves, muttering in the same voice, clustering round the gargantuan form of Ma Taproot. I guess they were worried. Making contingency plans. Fretting that their dreams were going awry.

My family members were plucking up their courage and moving towards us. They could see something was up. Something important.

Grandma was at their head, stumbling over the sandy rocks and looking worried. 'Lora, what's going on? What have they said?'

'It's okay, Grandma,' I said, still staring into Toaster's face. 'It's nothing bad. They've just told us they need Toaster's help, in order to take these ships into the stars.'

'What?' Grandma halted in her tracks. 'Are you kidding? They need my Servo? My loyal and faithful sunbed?'

She was sounding annoyed and I suddenly thought that she was going to mess everything up. She was going to insist that Toaster belonged to her and must do her bidding. Of course she wouldn't set him free to go wandering through space with the Ancients...

Even if it was the thing he most longed to do in the whole world.

And I knew it was.

It was about pure knowledge and adventure. Toaster

was tearing himself apart inside, trying to resist that temptation, for our sake.

Now Grandma was shouting across the hot sand at Ma Taproot.

'He's the only one who can fly these ships, is he, huh? Ha! Well, he's clever is Toaster. He always was! He's been brilliant, all our lives. Looking after us and making sure we're safe. We couldn't have asked for a better helper. He is a true member of our family.'

Toaster looked up and stared at Grandma.

'But now we have to say goodbye to him,' she said, in her gruffest voice. I knew she was trying not to cry.

Toaster said, 'I promised to protect the Robinsons forever.'

'We don't need you anymore,' said Grandma. 'We've had all the adventures and all the dangers we're ever going to get into. Right now we're gonna go back to the prairie and rebuild the Homestead and have a quiet life.'

'That is all I want, too,' said Toaster. 'To return to our old life.'

'No,' she grinned. 'You've learned everything you need to know about living that life. You've learned so much in the past couple of years, and you want … you *need* … to go on learning, don't you?' She patted his hard metal shell fondly. 'Well, it seems obvious to me what you've got to do.'

By now the rest of my family had arrived and they were gathering around the sunbed.

We all hugged him one at a time.

We were urging him to make his choice: Da, Ma, Hannah, Al, Peter.

'I actually have a choice?' Toaster asked. 'I'm free to choose?'

'Of course,' Da told him. 'You've always been free.'

Ma Taproot had come closer again. Her ancient, crumpled face was looking hopeful. 'Will you? Will you come with us to the stars?'

Toaster stared at everyone in turn. He turned lastly to Ma Taproot and considered her very carefully.

'Of course I will,' he said.

Everyone cheered. Our hearts would break to see him go, but still we cheered.

'And Lora,' Ma Taproot looked down at me with shining eyes. 'What about you? You would be most welcome to join us. You and your friends. All of them! We have enough room! Your whole family! Why not? What do you say? Will you return to the life you have known already, or will you come with us ... to *explore the galaxy*?'

I hesitated.

I really did hesitate.

For one long moment.

I felt the eyes of the Ancients upon me. Arnold squeezed my hand. I glanced back at my waiting family and friends.

Toaster never said a word. He knew this had to be my choice.

I said: 'There's been enough adventuring around these parts for now. I reckon it's time for us to go home.'

Ma Taproot nodded graciously and bent to kiss my cheek. Toaster saluted me with his clamp-like hand. I hugged his metal body one final time.

The Ancients gathered around me for a sort of clumsy group hug. I felt the collected warmth of their minds as they surrounded me. I felt I was held within the very Heart of Mars.

And then the whole lot of them simply melted away, taking Toaster with them. It was like they vanished in that wavering heat haze from the desert sand. And they were gone.

I was left standing alone under the shadow of the ships.

The air trembled and started to fill with the screaming of engines. They were powering up. They sounded more confident than before.

Around me my family and friends were talking all at once. I thought about Toaster aboard that ship. What was he thinking? How was he feeling? What was he going to be like without all of us to look after? And I thought: maybe I'll never find out what becomes of him next.

Then we were quiet for an awestruck moment, watching the Starships as they sailed grandly away out of Martian skies.

And then?

We had nothing but red prairie ahead of us, stretching out in all directions.

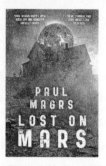

Book One of the Lora Trilogy
Lost on Mars
978-1-910080-22-1
£7.99

Book Two of the Lora Trilogy
The Martian Girl
978-1-910080-44-3
£7.99

Mr Ripley's Enchanted Books Top Favourite Book Reads 2015
'It's FANTASTIC, it's BRILLIANT, it's certainly strange and the plot will hit you in both the gut and the heart at the same time. It's thought provoking and very surreal … the more that I read, the more that I fell in love with this book… This is easily my favourite read of the year. It is a cracking space odyssey.'

The Independent's Best Summer Reads
'A wonderfully written sci-fi adventure about a pioneer family on the desert plains of the red planet, a terrifying, inhospitable world of massive dust storms. Then the disappearances begin. Grandma is taken and all that is left is her cybernetic leg. Completely irresistible.'
Patricia Duncker

'Paul Magrs's *Lost On Mars* is about Martian settlers being Disappeared by Martians. Funny, scary, and like Ray Bradbury crossed with Laura Ingalls Wilder, it will appeal to boys and Dr Who fans.'
Amanda Craig

Firefly

http://www.fireflypress.co.uk